A Murder Brings The Most Unlikely People Together

LILLIAN MISAR

Order this book online at www.trafford.com
or email orders@trafford.com

Most Trafford titles are also available at major online book retailers.

Printed in the United States of America.

ISBN: 978-1-4669-8673-2 (sc)
ISBN: 978-1-4669-8672-5 (e)

Trafford rev. 03/25/2013

Trafford
PUBLISHING® www.trafford.com

North America & international
toll-free: 1 888 232 4444 (USA & Canada)
phone: 250 383 6864 ♦ fax: 812 355 4082

PROLOGUE

SENNA AND CARLOTTA WERE shocked when the boss said he was taking them out to dinner and then a drive through the mountains on a sightseeing trip. Carlotta was thrilled, but Senna thought last week he took Mia and Tristen out and they never returned. He said "They transferred to a different gentlemen's club, more money, but Senna didn't believe him." She had been sick for two weeks and could not entertain the clients and Carlotta was so strung out on cocaine, the men didn't want her"

After dinner Damon drove them up a mountain road by a stream. He turned off into a small park with picnic tables. When he stepped on the brake, Senna sitting in the front saw a gun roll out from under the seat. He quickly shoved it back with his foot. She pretended not to notice.

There was melting snow on the ground, but it didn't seem cold. Damon said "Let's sit at a picnic table,

I brought a blanket so we can watch the water." Carlotta all dressed up took Damon's arm and swinging her hips walked with him to the table. They had both been told to dress up in their fancy clothes.

Senna saw the outdoor toilet down by the water and said she needed to use it. When she opened the door of the toilet, it shielded her as she hurled behind it into the ice cold rushing water. She tore off her fancy white jacket and stiletto heels sending them down the river.—then crouching—ran upstream.

Around a bend she had seen a place where the snow had melted by a treeline. Ahead was a mushy place with cattail plants. By now her feet were frozen and bleeding; she crawled in and covered herself with

1

leaves, dead grass, anything she could find. As she had ran upstream she had heard what sounded like a pop and then a scream. In her heart she knew Damon had shot Carlotta and rolled her up in the blanket he had brought to keep them warm. Soon she heard Damon yelling for her. She hoped he seen the coat and shoes going down stream. He would never believe that she would leave her beautiful coat and fancy shoes behind—she—hoped he would think she went downstream.

Senna lay still as a mouse until dark. She could see car lights shining down steam and a lot of yelling and swearing. She knew she had to get far away because he would call for help to find her. Desperate, an illegal alien, she was terrified to go to the police. She had heard they would throw her in jail—no—she had to somehow, get home to—Mexico—to tell everyone what happened to girls they took—supposed—to be good jobs in America. They were supposed to work as models—not as prostitutes.

CHAPTER 1

DANA PAINE A 55 year old widow, was having lunch with her three children at the local cafe in Placerville, South Dakota. Two of her married daughters and one in college were the light of her life —ESPECIALLY—her two grandchildren. She was looking out the window at the falling leaves and sighed"

I don't—think—I can stand another cold winter." One of the girls said "Ma" Why not try nursing down south, this winter? Lucy can stay in your house and go to college. Just try once, like take a leave of absence". Everyone chimed in, 'Yeah, try it, other people go south every winter, God, how long have you worked at the Care Center?" "Thirty years." "Well there you go, they will let you off for the winter. Call one of those labor places down south. We'll all get on the internet and look. Is your license valid in another state?" Dana's eyes lit up, "You know I think I will find out!"

Driving home Dana thought, why not, I'll start asking on Monday maybe there is some private nursing in Arizona—no—, maybe Texas. I think its warmer there. Lucy riding with her was chattering, like a magpie about college. She could live at home and save lots of money.

Monday morning found Dana at her usual 6:00 a.m. nursing job. It was still warm outside for October, but the winters in South Dakota are bad—20 to 30 below weather and lots of snow. All day while taking care of her patients—her mind was—whirling—on going south for the winter. A lot of her married friends had second houses in—Arizona, Texas and Florida. She knew she could not afford a second house—actually she knew she could not afford even, an apartment, unless she got a job there. The only drawback was

3

Christmas. Dana loved Christmas decorating inside and out, baking, having people over for parties.

People would drive by her house at night and honk their horns, just to let her know they loved her yard. She had a complete life size—nativity,—including camels and sheep that looked real.

The other side of her house, she had plastic penguins, on a layer of snow, in the summer it was a, tiered, landscaped rock garden full of bushes and flowers. The penguins stood in various poses by the bushes. She was already planning a new scene by her garage. Stop! she thought—one year won't matter—I want to try this down south thing.

After work she was going to take a nap, then thought, what the heck I'm going to call the Department of Labor. They said "Yes, her license would be valid in Texas." She made an appointment for the next day to visit a job placement clerk.

It was still nice out the next day when an excited Dana drove to another town to the Labor Office.

The clerk was very nice "Let's go on the internet and see what 1 can find." There were all kinds of listings for nursing homes and hospitals, a few private duty nurses, 24 hour jobs, in the clients or patient home. One stood out, a 75 year old man had broke his hip and needed around the clock care for at least three months and maybe longer. He lived on a ranch with his son and grandson who were busy with crops and livestock. They needed a cooking, housekeeping, nurse, the wages were open. Dana said "I could do that. I love to cook and clean and I'm a darn good nurse" "The job counselor took down all the information" Then tapping a few keys she was connected to the listed Texas office. Texas job service explained, "This man retired from ranching and after his wife died, took over the household duties and cooking and cleaning, whatever needed done". They did have a woman come in and help with washing clothes and taking care of the upstairs rooms for their hired men. The 75 year old fell off the roof breaking his hip and was depressed." Dana told them to give her a call if the family was interested in her credentials. On the way home Dana did wonder why no one in that area was interested in the job. She was relieved she had actually tried something so if it didn't turn out she still had a good job right here.

Making supper for her and Lucy she was dancing around singing Lucy laughed ", Mom you are such a nut. I hope you can do something different. It will be good for you to go somewhere besides South Dakota-" Later, they settled down to watch T.V., Dana reading the paper during cornmercials. When the phone rang they both jumped it was late. Lucy answered, a rnan asked for Dana Paine. Dana picked up the extension, "This is Hank Boldt, Jr.

""My Dad, Hank, Sr, broke his hip about a month ago. He up until then did the cooking and general gopher work around the place. My mother died about 5 years ago and he kind of retired to running the house" He is 75 and has become a bitter old man, won't even get out of bed some days. He refused physical therapy—ah—my sister stayed a week then my daughter another week". They have lives of their own so, we hired a nurse well-ah—it didn't work out. My Dad is a big man, 6 foot and some not so heavy, but hard to handle. My son and I lift him in and out of bed-ah—Mrs." Paine—ah, are you strong?"—,

Dana started to laugh, "Well, I stand almost 6 feet tall myself, I'm no light weight—not fat, but sturdy."

He went on uncomfortable," Well we live on an isolated cattle ranch. The last nurse lasted two days—well Dad ran her off! The one before refused to cook. We have a housekeeper, who lives with her husband here on the ranch, but Dad hates her cooking. She's Latino, ah, a lot of burrito's—spicy food—that's what she knows how to cook. Well anyway we need a big strong nurse that can cook and put up with a cranky old man. There is my son, me and a hired man living in the ranch house. I understand you want to be where it's warm. Your—ah—older so that would help Dad—ah—he kind of ran off the young nurse. Do you know anything about a cattle ranch?" Once again Dana laughed, "I was raised on a big cattle ranch in western South Dakota. I married a man from the eastern part of the state. He died five years ago of cancer.

So, I have plenty of experience lifting someone in and out of bed, plus dealing with angry, bitter people in a nursing home where I have spent almost all of my adult life and I want to spend a winter down South just once to try it out. "He said "wages ah—we need to talk wages. What do you earn now or—ah—I guess what you would expect, Rosa, our housekeeper takes care of a lot of the cleaning, but we do need someone to cook and take care of Dad." Dana," Well, I make

$3,600 a month now that includes insurance, but I have three months of benefits coming if I ask for a leave of absence, so I guess with room and board and some warm weather. How does $1,500 sound?' She could tell he breathed a sigh of relief. "You sound perfect for what we need, embarrassed, he said, "Are you white?" "Yes, "she laughed. He said, "We have lots of Mexican people here or Latinos—ah—"Are you prejudiced?" Once again, Dana went into peals of laughter, "No, we have lots of them here too. They work on the numerous dairy farms around me and their wives work at the nursing home with me. I'll tell you what—I will call you about 10:00 a.m. tomorrow after I talk to my boss. I think I could be there in a week, but not sure how he will take me asking for a leave of absence. I have been there thirty years so I might have a little struggle with him." "Wow, my Dad would respect that alone without hearing anything else about you."

The next morning Dana asked her boss when he came in at 9:00 a.m. At first he blew up and then finally said, "Well you can have three months and that's all. Let's see that would take until the middle of January." Then Dana bravely asked "I want to leave in a week." Then he did yell, she calmly explained the two young nurses at night want to come full time days. "I'll help you work out the schedule." He gave in after complaining a few more minutes. Exactly at 10:00 Dana called Hank Boldt. He answered on the first ring. "I can come next Monday. I hope that will work for you and I need to know where I fly or to what town?" He said, "Oh, I'll buy your ticket. We live about 60 miles from El Paso by a smaller town called Sunbird. Someone will pick you up In El Paso, where should I send your ticket?" "Make it Monday morning from Sioux Falls, South Dakota and you really don't have to buy my ticket." "Yes, yes, I want to. I have frequent flyer miles built up. We have our own plane, but I go to cattle shows in other states too far for our small plane, so I fly commercial, enough to get frequent flyer miles." Dana shocked, "You have your own plane? How big is your ranch?" "Ten thousand acres, it's pretty bare here. We raise sheep and cattle and of course, horses. Well, we are pretty isolated, the nearest town is twenty five miles away, Dad's doctor and the therapy he won't go to is there.

I sure hope you can drive—that is; if, we can ever get him to go."

Dana clearly amused by now," Yes, I can drive and this sounds like the perfect job for me." Hank relieved

"I will call with your plane reservations and you sound—like what we need." He called her back that night, and asked if she could leave by 6:00 A.M. next Monday, with one layover in Denver, Colorado, then on to El Paso. Would that work? "Dana thanked him, and then asked, "How warm it was there?" "Oh, it's terribly hot in the summer, but now it's about 75 to 80, once in a while it gets down to 50 at night or a little lower, not often."

For the next week a nervous Dana packed clothes, turned the utilities in her daughter's name and hoped she had not made a bad decision. She asked God to help her through this after all he had carried her through some bad times.

After a hectic week Dana was finally ready. Sunday night, Lucy and Dana drove to Sioux Falls and stayed at a motel. They went shopping, then on to a fancy restaurant, laughing and talking about everything under the sun. They were at the airport by 5:00 a.m., Dana wanted to make sure she was on time.

Her tickets were there and she convinced herself to calm down. She had chose a yellow pant suit with a sleeveless bright flowered blouse, she thought she could take the jacket off if it got to warm. Many hugs and kisses later she was finally on the plane. Dana quickly made friends on the plane, with her long black hair and twinkling brown eyes. People just naturally responded to her. In Denver several of her fellow passengers gave her advice as to how to maneuver from one gate to the next.

Dana hurried to find the El Paso gate. Ahead of her a young woman carrying a baby holding a little boys hand, while an older boy walked beside her. He kept looking back the way they had come. Dana thought,

Why is that child is terrified? What in the world? Just as they were all exiting the metal detector, a man rushed past and tried to grab the little boy, who then started screaming. The older child was desperately trying to hold on to his little brother, hitting at the man. Dana impulsive, grabbed the child screaming and the hand of the older boy and ran for all she was worth for the plane, the young mother sobbing behind her. Looking back Dana could see the security guards holding the man who was shaking his fist screaming profanities.

The little boy was hiding his head in Dana's shoulder and had a death grip on her hair. He refused to let go. Dana asked the hostess if they could somehow be seated together. The hostess observing, two sobbing children, a baby screaming it's head off and a terrified looking mother decided to put them all in a row of three seats. The oldest boy, rigid, tried to get the younger child to come to him. No way would the little guy let go of Dana's neck. Finally, settled haphazardly in a row, Dana holding the little boy on her lap, turned to the mother and kindly tried to put her at ease, she put her hand on the older boys shoulder. The baby seemed to sense everything was going to be alright as it quit crying. The mother, shaking so bad, could barely talk introduced herself—in jerky sentences. "I am—Lucia Montag. This, pointing to the baby, is Thomas. This is Joey, my four year old, who was still clinging to Dana and Josh my seven year old, turned adult because he has had to help me. I'm going home to my parents in El Paso. Obviously, my husband is furious." Dana said, "We will all get settled and then we can sort out who I am and why I'm going to El Paso. How's that sound?" Dana thought, Holy Cow! How did this happen? Oh well, I'll just have to be a wrinkled mess when I get there. This poor girl definitely needs help.

They were in the air when Lucia started talking, she said, "My husband beat me up in front of the children last night. Josh stepped in and he threw him across the room. I knew I had to leave for sure now as things have went from bad to worse. I can do nothing right to please this man. Now he is starting on the children belittling them in front of friends and relatives. I waited until he went to work this morning then grabbed a few things and called a cab. Somehow he must have found out I used a credit card for airline tickets. My Dad will have a fit. He is a well known attorney in El Paso and Catholic. He will try to make me come back, but I won't, I won't!" More tears. Dana horrified asked "What about your mother?" wiping her eyes Lucia, "I'm hoping she will stand up for me. I have bruises all over my stomach. When I fell on the floor he kicked me where ever it would not show. I'm still having trouble breathing, I think I'm just so scared. My mother is kind of a quiet, meek lady, but I think when I tell her the truth she will stop at nothing to help me even standing up to Dad, who is a stern man except when it comes to his grandchildren." Dana quietly, "Honey, all of us have to do what's best for our children and I couldn't help but see that they are afraid of their father."

After Joey fell asleep, Dana laid his head on a pillow in her lap. She asked Lucia to trade places with her so she could sit next to Josh, managing to hold Joey asleep. She started visiting with seven year old Josh. they visited for an hour about how stupid grown up people could be sometimes, then Dana told him about the many times she messed up as a mother and that her daughters had experiences like his. Pretty soon they were all laughing. Lucia put her seat back, the baby laying on her stomach, both fell asleep.

Dana and Josh held hands and watched a D.V.D that he had brought. After awhile they were all asleep except Dana. She prayed, "Dear God, please help this family."

When the baby woke up and cried, Dana carefully laid Joey down in her seat and asked the hostess if there was an empty two seats for her and Lucia farther back so they could feed the baby and talk.

Dana fed the baby his bottle while Lucia told her sad story. Dana asked if her parents knew she was coming? "They think it's for a visit." Dana hesitant, "Please go to an emergency room and get x-rayed as soon as we get there. I'm a nurse and I have noticed you wince every time you move. I didn't want the children to hear, You might have something broken, like a rib. I will tell you my tale now and we will keep in touch I want to hear everything about you and these beautiful children. I don't know how far I will be from El Paso but I will call you with the phone numbers and please if you need help with your father, I can tell him what I observed at the airport. Then Dana told Lucia all about her new adventure and she was a little nervous about this job, but was looking forward to warm weather.

When they landed there was a crowd of people standing by the gate, a Mexican or Latino man was holding a sign (Mrs. Dana Paine). Dana hurried over to him shaking his hand He said, "I'm Manuel Torres, Hank Boldt's hired man. I'm to drive you out to the ranch." She asked if he could watch for her luggage, it was marked with big black letters with her name. She wanted to say goodbye to someone she met on the plane." Dana walked over to the maybe Hispanic or Latino couple hugging Lucia. Lucia introduced Dana to her parents. Dana cut right to the chase, "I'm a registered nurse please go direct from here and take Lucia to a hospital emergency room. I believe she may have a broken rib and that can be very serious if it punctures a lung, I beg you!" Lucia's parents looked horrified as Lucia began to cry and then coughed. Still in a daze Lucia's father said "I'll go get the car. What the hell is going on here?" Dana said "Lucia I have your phone number and I will call you tonight, I did not want to scare you on the plane, but you need medical help."

CHAPTER 2

SENNA HAD LAID IN the nest she had made amongst the reeds and cattails. Now her feet were freezing she could no longer hear any noise. She still had her suit jacket on, but only stocking feet, she thought she could at times hear cars over a hill above her.

Carefully going from tree to tree making sure she didn't step in snow, she came to the top of the hill, overlooking a road houses and a lake. She could see lights in some of the houses, most were dark and one no smoke comes from the roof. She had to get warm, her teeth were chattering and her whole body was staring to shake.

She climbed down the steep hill dashing across the road to the dark house with no smoke. She prayed Heavenly Father, please help me out of this mess I have made of my life. I wanted more than my family was able to provide, yes I tried to be something I'm not. God help me!

On her hands and knees she desperately searched for a key to the garage door, turning over every rock, praying no one would see her. She stopped and looked at an owl statue, it's head looked funny. The head came off and there were the keys.

She opened the door to the garage and prayed. God let this key open the house door, it did. She could see an old car in the garage, like Mama's car. She sort of just slid into the house. it was cold, but better than outside that was for sure.

She found a kitchen; moonlight was now helping her find her way around the house. She waited for her eyes to adjust. Oh, a kitchen stove—electric—Oh, Thank you God, and she turned on the burners and the oven and then lay on the floor in a heap. Sobbing from the pain in her frozen joints and relief she laid a while. She found a can of peaches and an opener she gulped down the juice. The sweet peach juice running down her elegant dress and her beautiful face, now filthy dirty. Her hands and nails were full of dirt. She found the bathroom just to relieve herself brought on more tears and scrubbing her skin and nails. She was surprised there was water and then realized it was really not that cold in the house.

She started looking around the house; the living room overlooked the lake. She found a small flashlight, shinning it at pictures on a T.V. Shocked she found a family picture of a Latino family, a man wife and two children. Other pictures were just of a man and the two children.

Horrified but desperate she started searching for keys to the car in the garage. They were in the ignition, The back seat of the car had child carseats and fishing poles. She knew she had to hurry, what to do, she finally got in started the car and it started right up.

Back in the house she went to the bedroom with her little light looking for at least shoes and a different coat. She could find no women's clothes, just men and little kids. The flashlight suddenly flashed on a box in the closet, Lila's things, it said. What in the world, here was an entire box of clothes exactly Senna's size. Once again she slumped to the floor praising God. Dear Jesus if you will continue to help me out of this mess I will work with Mama cleaning toilets anything. She could still see her mother standing outside their poor farmhouse crying as she drove off in Damon's van to be a model. Ha! a model—right! The fancy women he had teach her better English and how to dress and walk only to find herself locked in a house with a tall fence all around it like a prison to be nothing but a whore. Men coming day and night, most of the girls on drugs. At least one man had stuck a $100 bill in her hand just to look at her naked, disgust; revulsion overwhelmed her for a minute until once again the anger came.

"How could I know. We were so poor. Lupe tried to raise chickens, pigs, goats and crops on their little farm, but it was not enough. Her poor Mother had to clean rooms at a fancy hotel, driving her old car, praying it would hold together another day." Senna had believed, no, wanted to believe, she could send money home. Damon said he was sending money to her mother every month, but she now knew better. Two months she had been locked in, never to see a dime except the

$100 bill pinned to her underwear, that she still had to help her with this escape. No, if she had to steal food, clothes and these peoples car, she would. Some day she would pay them back. Someday, she gritted her teeth, eyes flashing she would pay back Damon too, only not in a good way.

She put on the other woman's clothes and found the button for the garage door, opening a crack she started the car. it had a full tank of gas. Carefully she went outside to see if the car would leave tracks in the frost on the driveway. She saw a sack of ice melt; she covered the pavement with it. The car running she searched the house for food, a loaf of bread in the deep freeze and some lunch meat—and what in the world—a potato chip can in a deep freeze. Inside was a credit card with a piece of paper with the word pin on it. She knew how it was used because she had seen Damon using one and then punching in numbers. Anger, disgust with herself, "I am now a burglar, crying softly, what else can I do but steal?"

Opening the garage door as she had seen Damon's fancy lady teaching friends do, she found the thing in the car to shut the door. With no lights on she drove out to the road, legs and hands shaking so bad she could hardly drive. Which way right or left?? Trying to calm down she thought I must go east. "I'm sure I seen a sign for Bullhead, Arizona when Damon brought us up here, but where was east? Looking through the windshield she spotted the big dipper in the sky, with a sigh of relief, she thought—right—it has to be to the right. Still no lights on the car she carefully drove down a hill, a few houses had lights on.

She decided most of the houses were actually summer cabins for rich people. Although the name on the credit card she stole was Gary Valdez, who looked Hispanic. She decided him to be very rich, and hoped with all her heart he would not prosecute a fellow countryman. Winding down hills around curves she started to relax her grip on the steering wheel, with the lights on she felt safe for a few miles. She had to get somewhere far away and then call Father John. He would find a way to get her brother and get her home. Tears started running down her face when she saw the sign Bullhead Arizona, only it was a highway with a lot of traffic even though it was midnight. "Could she drive across Arizona in a stolen car??"

CHAPTER 3

MANUEL STOOD WATCHING THIS tall sophisticated looking lady hugging, none other than Don Santigo's daughter, at least it sure looked like the famous lawyer. He thought "Oh boy, she don't look like no ranch person to me, Mr. Boldt's not going to like this!" Just then his cell phone rang. Mr. Buck asked, "Did you find her?" "Yeah boss, she's tall long black hair and dressed fit to kill—Ah-, I don't know she kinda bounces when she walks-and ah, she's hugging Don Santigo's daughter and kids, I don't know what to think!"

Buck swearing, "What is she doing with Santigo's, I hope to hell I didn't pay for a damn plane ticket for nothing—you say Don Santigo—What the hell?"

About then Dana hurried over to Manuel and said, "Oh .... God I'm so sorry to hold you up! Let me carry one of those suitcases. I did not know what to pack." Manuel hung up the phone. He said "I will go get the car, you can wait right here." When he got her luggage in the car and then opened the door for her, she laughed, "Good grief I did not expect to be treated like a fancy lady."

Manuel behind the wheel, "We have a long drive ahead of us. Is there any place you would like to stop?" Eyes twinkling, Dana says "Coffee and where can I have a cigarette—I need one!" "Well ma'am, we can smoke in the car, we'll roll down the windows .... Okay? We can go to a drive-up for coffees. Will that work?"

Dana asked to get out of the car at the coffee place for just a few minutes. She got out of the big Cadillac and turned in a complete circle. At the same time taking off her jacket, laughing, "It was fifty degrees when I left South Dakota.—What is it here?" Manuel watching her said, "Ah, eighty I think." "Oh, my! I love it!" They got their coffee and started out.

Manuel started hesitantly explaining why they had to not waste time, "My wife is fixing dinner for our Mr. Hank today—ah—he's really crabby, demanding chicken and dumps or something dumb like that. My Rosa don't know how to cook this and she is all upset, crying and everything." Dana slapped her leg and burst out laughing, "Yes, I can cook chicken and dumplings. He sounds like a holy terror. I like feisty old people. No one is going to take advantage of them."

After finally driving out of the town Manuel finally got up nerve enough to ask," How she knew Don Santigo?" She said "Who? Oh you mean at the airport, I didn't know his name, I helped his daughter through a nasty mess. She told Manuel the story from beginning to end." Manuel awestruck "Dear God in Heaven, he's the most famous attorney in El Paso and you think he won't help his daughter because their Catholic! Well, damn excuse me—that's just not right—my God I'm Catholic and nobody better not beat up on my daughter!" For a few minutes you could tell Manuel was mulling this information over in his mind.

Finally he asked her about South Dakota. What it was like? Were there lots of Indians? She said, "Well, the eastern half is lush, green country, but terrible cold. The western half is dry prairie land except for the Black Hills. I have lived in the east for thirty years, but I was born and raised in the western ranch country, where even trees don't grow, but cattle thrive on the buffalo grass.

"Manuel pointed out all the sights until they got out to the flat country. Looking at her," It's pretty dry, dusty and isolated out to the ranch; we don't get much rain here. Well—ah—it looks like you came from a nice place, I'm not sure if you will like it here." She really laughed then, "Honey, I was raised with no running water in a stucco house, poverty stricken, but I never knew we were poor until I left home. So you are telling me what? Oh, I get it. I've scratched out a living for my kids and myself. I divorced my first husband, who was a farmer. The second husband died soon after I married him so I had to move to town with my girls. I have struggled all my life with money. I have a modest home paid for and a new car, but that's about it."

He breathed a sigh of relief," Well darn it, you sure look well, pretty and rich for a proper mature nurse, like Mr. Hank wants. I was kind of worried when I first seen you. Now I'm a thinking, your just right, yep, just right. The young pretty nurses we had wouldn't do nothing, but flirt with Sid—Bucks son-." "Who's Buck?" "Oh, that's Hank, Junior—Old Hank started calling him that when he was a kid and the name just stuck."

Dana," Stop!—Along side of the road was a huge lumbering animal—is that an armadillo?—Wow I have never seen one even in a zoo?" "Ma'am, don't get out. There might be a rattlesnake!" She shook her whole body, "And those I hate if I never see another rattlesnake in my life I could be so happy!!" "Oh, don't look like that—I know there's rattlesnakes here. I already looked that up. Now I want to see a real road runner."

By the time they came over a hill overlooking a valley Manuel and Dana were old friends. Far off she could see the ranch. Sitting forward, she said," But it's beautiful. Are those trees and a creek or river?" "It's dry now, but when it rains there's water. There are mesquite and two huge pecan trees by the house. Mr. Hank always kept it mowed; Buck and the rest of us don't have time. So, everything is looking-ah—a little tough." The ranch house sat up on a hill—barns below. It was a big log and brick, around the bottom, with steps leading up to a front porch. A front porch was clear across the front of the house with chairs and tables for sitting scattered here and there. The grass was tall but off to the right looked like a garden and two big trees. The house had been landscaped at some time, big bushes in rock around the outside, and a split rail fence by the driveway." Wow," Dana said, "Wow, it's a big place!",

CHAPTER 4

ABOUT 10:00 P.M. DAMON got back to his apartment—wet from running through the grass and trees at the park. His dress shoes and suit pants were ruined. He was furious. He changed clothes, and then still chilled he called his head security guard. "George, we have a problem!" George appeared to be a big lumbering easy going man, unless you crossed him, than the evil showed. Damon thought they were friends, George secretly despised him. He was paid good money so whatever Damon wanted he did. George said, "What happened?'" "Senna ran off. I think she jumped in the creek and tried to go downstream. I found her shoe and blanket by the bridge, out at the park, the dumb bitch, must have hit the deep water below the bridge, where the rapids are. I hunted for hours. Get Lonnie up and tell him we are leaving at daylight in the morning." George called Lonnie, "We have a problem. Damon was doing his F—shit again. He did Carlotta, but Senna got away. He wants us early in the morning up at the lake to look for her." Lonnie sleepy, What?" Damon is a F—psychopath! I'm not helping him find anyone. I don't want to know what that s.o.b. is doing ever!!!" George listened, "You like the money though don't you Lonnie—huh?" Lonnie sputtered, "Yeah, but Senna, Why Senna? She is so beautiful." "Well" George said," We think she has been stealing food from the kitchen at night even raw potatoes. She is one smart little girl. She must have caught onto the drugged food. Then we think she played sick for two weeks until she could figure out a way to get away. She was too clever for her own good." Lonnie yelling, "Look we are going to get in trouble that Damon is a loose cannon. Someone will find a body someday; I don't want any part of this! What's he do with them—Oh God—don't tell me—I don't like this business at all!"

George in a calm menacing voice, "There's an old well up there, that's where Damon's people come from; the rest you don't need to know."

Daybreak the next morning found the three of them walking upstream and then downstream where they found Senna's other shoe about a mile from the bridge. Lonnie insisted they get the hell out here before someone seen them. What they didn't know was someone did see them. When Mr. Ring came home for lunch, his wife Clara said," Guess what? I saw Damon Hutt again, this morning, up in the park!" Her husband groaned," Again, Clara you're losing your mind. He's some big shot in Las Vegas. His folks have been gone for years. What in the world would he be doing up here?" I know it was him, I got the binoculars out—he was standing on the hill—I looked right into his cold blue eyes. He was a monster when he was a kid and I just know it, he's still a monster." She shivered.

CHAPTER 5

Rosa came running out to meet Dana and Manuel. Manuel introduced Dana to Rosa. She said "Am I ever glad to see you, I've had it with that old fart!"

On the porch floor a big what looked like a coon dog was flopped. The dog didn't move. Dana said to the comatose dog, "And what's your name?" he raised his big head and then fell back to sleep. Rosa, "That's Bo Jangels and he's the best snake dog in this country. He hates snakes." "So do I!" laughed Dana. Rosa wringing her hands," Mr. Hank is being a holy terror today; he says my chicken and dumps are all wrong." Dana went to meet her new patient, who lay in a hospital bed. A big white-haired—strong face—no wrinkles. Dana thought, good grief John Wayne, good grief. He hollered when he seen her," God damn it! Where's my food? Are you the one that supposedly can cook? I'm so sick of Mexican food I could scream and I need to go to the bathroom, I couldn't go until Manuel came. What a crock of shit no one really cares if I live or die." "Hello, hello, Dana said, setting her purse on the floor. She found a gait belt, sat him up and had his feet on the floor before he knew what happened. She grabbed a wheelchair—lifted him carefully off the bed and wheeled off to the bathroom—up and on the toilet, without saying a word. All the time he was glaring at her.

Dana said, "Now tell me about this chicken and dumpling deal. Do you make them with cream?" He said "Damn right and their fluffy, you ought to see what Rosa made, for God's sake there like lumps of lead—shit—shit!" Dana laughing, hands on her knees said, "You poop while I make some new dumplings, then you come out to the table and eat." "I'm not coming out anywhere. I eat in my room!" "Ha! She said, with her twinkling laugh—you are at my mercy now—young man—so you will do what I say." Then laughing she hurried to the kitchen—where Rosa and Manuel stood in shock.

Dana carefully took the lumps off the chicken—asking Rosa to find her the ingredients—she made a new batch of dumplings—putting a lid on the pan setting the timer for ten minutes. She asked Rosa, What else was she planning for dinner?" Rosa said, "I made a loaf of frozen bread and a salad he insisted I put bacon grease on. Oh my, he shouldn't have that!" Dana went, "Oh poof, I called his doctor yesterday for his orders. He said let that old buzzard do what he wants—just get him on his feet." Rosa put her hands on her head covering her eyes, "Well, good luck getting him to do anything besides bitch!"

By then old Hank was bellowing from the bathroom, "GET ME OFF." By then Dana had found a pair of sweat pants and a sweat shirt—a pair of boxer shorts. When she walked in the bathroom with all the clothes, he went ballistic," Woman can't you see, I can't wear clothes—I'm an invalid—besides I never wore that kind of stuff in my life and I'm not going to start now!!" Dana on her knees put his feet in the boxers and sweat pants—then unbuttoned his pajama top and pulled a sweat shirt over his head—all the time talking a mile a minute about how she was here to get him on his feet and he damn well better get used to it. Then Dana put her hands on her hips and burst out laughing at his antics. "Mr. Hank, you are going to eat at the table with us and then—guess what—we are going outside to that veranda or porch and have coffee—a cigar for you and a cigarette for me and you are going to take your pain pill—because we start therapy tomorrow—your doctor says." Looking at her trying to scowl, "Woman I can't take pain pills they constipate me. I'll never walk again. Why go through all that misery?" Yelling now, "Damn people don't know what pain I'm in and what do you mean you're the boss. I'm paying you, or did you forget that?" While he was blowing off, Dana was lifting him into his wheelchair. To his surprise he looked at her with new respect, "How the hell did you do that? I didn't feel a thing???" She hugged him, "I love you already and your right I don't know your pain, but I can keep you from being constipated and I damn well can get you on your feet—count on it—count on it."

She pushed him, in his wheelchair out to the table—where Rosa and Manuel stood their mouths wide open with shock. Dana took the chicken and now fluffy dumplings off the stove and asked Rosa and Manuel to stay for dinner. After they were all settled Rosa asked, "How do you get fluffy dumps?" "Oh, the key is to never take the lid off the pan even if it boils over." Dana started asking questions about all their lives. Rosa explained, "She lived behind the big house on the other side of the trees, a nice house. Hank provided for them—looking at Manuel—she went on—we have lived here all our married life—Manuel was born here." Hank started telling about Manuel's folks working for him until Manuel got married. His folks retired and moved to town. Damn, woman these are the best chicken and dumplings I have had since my wife died. Well, hell you're a keeper even though your pretty damn bossy, Nurse Paine, the name sure as hell fits and your too old to fall in love with Sid like those other dingbats. God, what I have been through I'm used to being busy—look at this yard—everything is a mess—Rosa tries to keep up, but she's got three young ones and another on the way!" Rosa blushed. "I can't keep up with the garden—you—this big house—hanging her head, I'm sorry." Hank said, "You have done a damn good job. I'm sorry I've been such an ass!" Tears came to Rosa's eyes. Dana laughed, "Hey, I'm here—you're the boss except on your medical care—get that straight—otherwise I will do what you tell me needs to be done. Okay?" Hank finally laughed, a deep hearty laugh, "Can I really have a cigar and coffee?"

They left the dishes, Dana pushed him outside. Manuel and Rosa pulled up chairs. The old coon dog jumped up and laid on Hanks feet. Hank told Dana all about the ranch—his son—his grandson—and the other hired man. Rosa and Manuel chimed in with stories of their own. Dana listened with interest to telling until Hank said, "What about you Missy?" Dana laughed, "I'll tell you quick like some of my life and then I had better unpack and find out what you want for supper."

Manuel and Rosa jumped up, "We'll show you your room." It was a big house, huge kitchen just off the porch—a living room off to the left—all open big cathedral ceilings—a huge fireplace—down a long hallway there was an open staircase. They took her past Hanks bedroom to a smaller room with a walk in closet-bare wood floor—a

21

large bed and plain dresser was in sight, but then Dana clapped her hands in delight—there was a patio door leading outside to a screened in porch—overlooking a lawn and then a path going through some bushy like trees. Rosa pointed out—that was the way to their house. "Oh, wow, Dana said, "This is wonderful."

"Hank looking tired, "Ah—could I get back in bed first before you settle in—Rosa will find what you need and Manuel can help you get me in bed." Dana with her tinkling laugh, "I can get you in bed and we will practice right now while Manuel is still here." Dana lowered the bed and turned to Hank who was grimacing, "It hurts so bad I just dread getting up." Dana—"Okay—now—you and I are going to hug—hold on to me tight—I'm going to put my knee between your legs and the next thing he knew he was in bed." Relief in his face, "How did you do that? It didn't hurt." Dana jumped around "Aha,—I told you, ring that bell if you need me and what do you want for supper, and how much and what sounds good?" "Can you make goulash? I'm so hungry for that." Dana, "How do you make it, it might be different then my version?" "Write this down that should feed all of us tonight and strawberry shortcake—Oh God—how much I miss that." Dana wrote down his directions then Rosa said," She would round up all the ingredients—while Dana got settled.

Manuel left—Rosa showed Dana the rest of the house—a huge all open stairway —right in the middle of the house—with beautiful details. Dana and Hanks bedroom down on the right side of the stairs, on the other side was another bedroom and a bathroom. The bedroom on the right side of the stairs looked as if was an office with a bed in it.

That's Buck's office we moved his bed dresser and stuff so you could have his room. He would sleep upstairs except he needs to watch over Mr. Hank at night."

Dana couldn't help noticing the whole house needed a good scrubbing, but she wisely kept that to herself, saying," Rosa do you do the men's rooms upstairs too? How in the world do you keep up?" Rosa, a tired look on her face, "I can't keep up—I'm trying but there is just too much." Dana said, "I will do what you can't, but me tell please if I'm stepping on your territory or your toes." Rosa looked at her feet. Dana slapped her knee and laughed, "Oh, I mean if I stick my nose in your business." Rosa, Cleaning and cooking were not my job until

Mr. Hank got hurt. He did everything, but the upstairs rooms. I clean them and wash the bedding, for the hired men and Sid."

After Rosa showed Dana the stuff for supper, Dana told her," You go home if you want—we'll be finejust leave your phone number." Rosa breathed a sigh of relief.

CHAPTER 6

MANUEL CALLED BUCK ON his cell as soon as he started out to the field. Buck, "Yo, how did it go? Sorry I didn't have time. What's she like? A dragon lady, I hope or otherwise the old man will never get well." Manuel snorted, "I don't know about dragon—she laughs all the time. When we got home Mr. Hank had Rosa in tears. The nurse just took over—she lifted him out of bed—to the bathroom—dressed him—and made fluffy dumps or something—all in about twenty minutes. She made him take a pain pill and come out to the table to eat. Then she told him—tomorrow, you start therapy. I called your doctor, from home yesterday—he gave me your information—Okay?"

Buck incredulous, "What tell me all that again? She must be one tough old lady." Manuel, "Well—ah—not so old—she is one good looking lady—tall—not big, but well. sturdy. I think she is about your age—When I left Mr. Hank was ordering her around what to make for supper—Rosa was helping her find stuff she needed for goulash or some damn thing, and I guess I should tell you this—after dinner she pushed your Dad's wheelchair out on the porch—got him a cigar and coffee, and then she had a cigarette—ah—you might think her wrong, but she says, "Doctor said to just get him back on his feet whatever it takes."

Buck astonished," Well, for crying out loud—did you help her get him back in bed?" "No sir, she does it by herself and he says it didn't hurt. I guess I think she's about—ah—the best nurse I ever seen!

One thing though—when she got off the plane—she was with Don Santigo's daughter—you know that big shot lawyer—I can't get my mind around this—in Denver or some city—the daughter's husband tried to run through security to grab one of his kids—the kid was screaming his head off—scared to death of his Dad—so it seems our nurse grabbed the kid and ran behind the mother into the plane—and the mother was terrified her Dad would make her go back because they're—Catholic—Damn that made me mad—when she told me—our nurse told old Don he needed to take the daughter to a hospital—the look he gave our nurse—oh boy. It didn't seem to bother Nurse Paine at all. If anything she talks a lot, about wore me out coming home with questions.

She—oh'd and ah'd—over her bedroom with the patio outside. She loved. . . . . it. I'll start cutting hay down here—okay? Oh God I about forgot all this—she told Mr. Hanks he's the boss except his medical care, and then she's the boss. She's kind of like a damn whirlwind.

I guess she really hates snakes—so old Bo Jangles laid on Mr. Hanks feet on the porch. He told her he was a snake dog—she got down on her knees—put her hands on either side of Bo's head—and said—let me think—yeah—"Where thou goest I shall follow, you will be my Savior." Bo looked at her like she was nuts—then thumped his tail—then she asked for a big leaf rake—I brought it to her—she says she will use it around the garden cause Rosa told her there's a nice garden, but not time to take care of it. Dana told Rosa when the kids get home from school—they maybe could all go to the garden. Oh, one more thing I forgot, Martha's home, she called and talked to the old man that sure perked him up. The nurse asked him to have her come to supper because he said he likes how Martha does cucumbers. That's about it boss. I'm going to the field."

Buck thought to himself when he hung up, Manuel was really wound up. What the hell, was all that about, I can't believe it.

Dana changed into Levis and a white tank top that said nurse on it. She looked in the oven, it was filthy, grabbing some paper towels and vinegar, she thought, how can I bake a cake in this dirty oven. Do I have time for the self cleaner? She quit scrubbing and turned the oven to clean for two hours. Then she looked in the laundry and mudroom combination right of the kitchen. There was piles of laundry on the floor so she had to climb over them to get to the washer. She dug around until she found an entire load of dingy white laundry. She started the washer and made an attempt at cleaning up the kitchen.

She stopped to call her daughter-Lucy-using her cell phone outside. She told her it's a beautiful house, but oh my, it's dirty, for a few minutes I didn't know where to start. Lucy laughed, "Oh Ma, that's just your cup of tea—cleaning-you love it. What's the old man like?" Dana talked for thirty minutes, talking as fast as she could, until the washer shut off. She hung up and started another load of laundry.

She took all the breakfast food boxes off the middle island counter in the kitchen and found a whole empty cupboard—for all the stuff sitting on the kitchen counters. She went to the deep freeze sitting in the garage and found it full of meat and vegetables. She found several packages of frozen strawberries.

Hank hollered from the bedroom, "What the hell smells?" Dana ran in to his room, "I'm cleaning the oven, I'm sorry, I'll open a window." He mellowed out, "Nah—the house is dirty, I know, Rosa is wonderful, easy going, kind, but not much of a housekeeper. My Lizzie kept everything so clean. I guess we kind of all let things go." Dana said, "Oh no, it's not that bad. I like to clean. I asked Rosa if she cared what I did and she seemed relieved to have me—ah—take over. Please don't let me offend you—tell me if I'm out of line. Hank snorted, "My guess is you're a damn bulldozer—offend me—hell—you do what you can to clean things up. Hey, can you run a riding lawn mower?" "You betcha, that's tomorrow—okay? Rosa and the kids are coming over to help me get some stuff out of the garden."

About then Rosa called from the back door—three children in tow—she introduced them—Mikala is thirteen—then Joseph is eleven—Luke is seven. "I brought oatmeal cookies for lunch." All of them holding their noses, "What's that smell?" Dana explained, and then they had cookies and milk. Dana brought Hank lunch—he rolled his eyes at the rock hard cookies—twinkling bright blue eyes he said, "See what I mean?"

Rosa and the kids brought out their pails and they headed for the garden. Dana grabbed her leaf rake and woke up Bo—come she said. The old dog stretched, finally ambling along in front of Dana. Rosa and the kids giggled. Dana said, "Laugh all you want. I hate snakes!" Manuel had packed straw around all the plants, so it wasn't a weed patch like the yard. There were luscious tomatoes and cucumbers galore. Rosa found some summer squash remarking how Mr. Hank loved it, but she couldn't get it right for him-so they gathered squash too. Dana visiting with the kids about school, laughing and talking, by now all of them made the hot work fun. Dana a put a sweat band on her head, she knew she looked ridiculous, but not used to the heat yet. On the way back to the house she stopped, "Are those pecans on the ground? Oh my, are they ready to pick?" "Oh yes," from Rosa, "it takes so long though." Dana looked longing at the pecans then decided she had better get back to the house, get this cake baked and supper ready.

She asked Rosa, "How did she sort the clothes for the men?" Rosa showed her each man had a basket. Mihala started emptying the dryer and folding underwear, each man's name was on their clothes. Dana threw in another load of shirts. Rosa watching amazed," How did you get them so white?" Dana, "I squirted in some dawn dish soap, it seems to help. Can we hang these shirts up on hangers on that rod above the washer? Is that how you do it?" Rosa smiling, "No, I throw them all in a basket, but they should be hung up—the washing gets ahead of me—I can't keep up." Dana hugged Rosa, "Please let me help—I don't have three kids just one big one in bed." Everyone laughed then pitched in to fold clothes even the boys.

CHAPTER 7

SENNA STOPPED AT A truck stop along the highway—terrified she had
to go to the bathroom and she needed coffee or pop something with
caffeine. She went inside and asked if she had to pay before pumping
gas—trying to look normal she asked for a cash machine—the nice
older clerk pointed to an ATM and said, "We like people to pay
before they pump." Senna's hand was shaking as she inserted Gary
Valdez's card in the slot. The machine asked for a pin she punched in
the numbers stuck to the back of the card—immediately the machine
asked the amount. She chose one hundred dollars and nearly fainted
when five twenty dollar bills popped out. Her insides felt like jello, but
she knew she must act calm. Going back to the clerk Senna gave her
forty dollars—then asked for a cup of coffee and a roll and a map.

Senna asked, "How far to Phoenix?" The clerk said, "It's about
forty miles." Senna went out and pumped her gas then lifted the hood
and checked the oil. She went back inside for her coffee and roll no
one seemed to be paying any attention to her. She asked the clerk,
"Where she could buy a cell phone or something so she could call
home as her mother was sick and she was going home to be with her."
The lady said, "We don't have cell phones, but you could buy a calling
card for regular phones, sometimes cell phones don't work. I'm sorry
about your mother and hope you get home all right.

Be kind of careful out on the highway there's always stuff going on
in the dark hours it seems." Senna started to leave and then went back
in and asked if the traffic was bad by Phoenix. "Yes, real bad between
7:00 and 9:00 a.m.

Senna got back in the car still scared but, felt a little safer now
if she could just get through the traffic and get a calling card or

something. She was afraid she would have to have I.D. to buy a cell phone—what to do?? She drove off it was still early in the morning maybe she should bypass Phoenix and go south to Tucson, Arizona. She started feeling calmer—her mind working again—yes—if she stayed on the freeway—she could bypass Phoenix and Tucson was a lot closer to home. She decided to call Father John at lunch time he should be home then maybe he could call the border guards at the gate and help her get through with no I.D. She thought most important that she not get caught in this country. They would throw her in jail for sure. She thought—bus—I can take a bus—yes—from Tucson—leave this car there and have Father John call him only after she got over the border and tell Mr. Gary Valdez that she would pay him every penny she owed him. She felt bad that she had got herself in such a mess, but decided to leave her pride behind and ask or beg for help.

Ahead she seen a sign Tucson—90 miles—over and over she thanked God. By now she had seen police cars and no one seemed interested in her at all. Senna stopped at another truck stop and bought a sandwich and made sure the car was full of gas. She took out one more $100.00 from Gary's card—she might need more money. She had no idea what a calling card would cost. She was still terrified, but all she had to do was think of Damon and that seemed to give her courage to go. Really scared now she could see the outskirts of Tucson—what exit to take—God help me—she turned off and nearly yelled out loud when she seen a Wal-Mart sign.

Now how to get there? Her heart was beating a mile a minute, she was so excited —she did it—she did it—Thank You God.

CHAPTER 8

DANA WENT TO THE bedroom with another pain pill for Hank and told him tomorrow they would buy the stuff to make fruit soup—did he know what that was?" "I sure do my mom used to make it—Oh—that will keep me from getting constipated—well, darn, I should have thought of that.—Ah—nurse Paine—is it possible for you to help me get kind of gussied up before Martha gets here?" Dana searched the closet and found western dress pants and a fancy western shirt. She helped him to the bathroom, so he could hold on to the rails while she fixed him up. He looked so handsome—thick white hair—bright blue eyes-he looked like a rich rancher, maybe that's what he was. Dana put him in his wheelchair and asked him to come out and supervise the goulash.

She hurried up and wiped out the oven. Rosa had found an old angel food cake mix and an old angel food pan—Dana used that, while Rosa cut up the squash. Hank was thrilled he wanted brown sugar and butter—real butter—on the squash. Dana put everything in the oven. Rosa filled the washer again with Levis and looked at the time—we have to go—can you manage?"

Martha got there about 5:30 p.m. hugged and kissed a blushing Hank. Dana smiled, "Martha, you're a blessing—can you do these cucumbers how he wants them and the tomatoes?" Dana ran back to the dryer and got the damp shirts out; Mikala had gone to all the rooms and gathered hangers. Martha got the dishes out of the dishwasher and set the table, all the time visiting while she worked about staying with her daughter for a month helping with a new baby granddaughter.

By 6:30 Dana asked," Is everything under control? Can we go outside and have a —what—ah—a cocktail?" "Sure", Hank had a beer, Martha and Dana found a bottle of wine. Dana sat down, blowing wet sweaty strands of hair off her face. "Wow, time to sit down that's for sure."

The three were relaxing on the porch when two pickups drove up. Sid was the first one on the porch. My God, Dana thought he looks like Tom Cruise. He gave his Grandpa a big bear hug picked Martha up, sitting her down, he yelled, "Hey Dad, Pete, the old man's up, what in the world made you finally decide to live?" All three men stood in front of Hank and cheered. Buck was a tall dark-haired man—sharp blue eyes. Pete was a tall Mexican man very attractive both men. Each man turned to Dana—Sid shook her hand saying," I'm the grandson; this is my Dad, Buck and our faithful servant—Pete. Pete snorted and punched Sid's arm." Buck came over to Dana shaking her hand too, "Well Nurse Paine I'm damn glad to see you, I was hoping I didn't buy a plane ticket for nothing, I sure can tell already your just right. Manuel went so far as to say, you are a keeper, you sure impressed him." Dana laughed her tinkling laugh, "Wait until after supper, and then tell me. Your Dad supervised, but I'm not sure." The men all had on cowboy hats and western shirts with the sleeves cut off. They all got a beer and then joined everyone on the porch. They all asked Dana about her trip.

She jumped up, "Oh my, I forgot to whip the cream, I found all kinds of stuff in the fridge, supper will be soon." When she left Hank made a prayer like shape with his hands, "I hope the food Gods is good to me and I hope I can keep Nurse Paine forever even though, she is a pain in the butt." When they heard the mixer running Sid said, "Wow, she's a good looking lady." Buck said, "Son, she's a little old for you." Everyone laughed —Sid not bothered a bit," She's not too old for you—old man!" Martha went in to help Dana. Sid said, "What about you Gramps—did you get all fixed up for the new nurse or Martha?" Everyone laughed.

The working men all washed up while Martha and Dana put supper on the table. Later Hank said, "I think I died and went to heaven. This is the best eats I've had for a long time—well ever since Martha didn't feel sorry for us and left for a long month." A lot of talk at the table, everyone so pleased to have Hank out of his room.

Dana got up to cut the cake. Martha helping her said, "Girl, how in the world did you make this perfect angel food cake. I've been baking for 75 years and never had one turn out like this." Dana flushed happy stopped in her tracks, "Seventy five years old, you can't be, and sorry but this is a box cake." Martha said, "No matter my box cakes don't turn out like this." Dana thought what a delightful old lady, my word, with her tanned face, arms and legs; even her feet in little sandals were tan. She had soft blonde hair and eye makeup—dressed in white Capri's and a pink polo top—tucked in—well she looked like a Barbie Doll. Out loud Dana told Martha exactly what she just thought. Martha looked pleased.

After Martha left Dana got Hank ready for bed—Buck came in to help lay him down. Hank said, "Let her do it. She knows how to do it so it don't hurt." After he was settled, Buck and Dana went out to the porch and visited. Dana asked him all about his work. He was surprised she knew so much about putting up hay. Dana headed for bed she was exhausted—threw off her Levis and fell into bed thinking I'll take a shower in the morning.

The next morning she was up early, showered—put her hair up on her head—makeup and a white nurse uniform. She hurried to Hank's room—helping him in a shower chair—then dressing him in his good clothes. He grumbled half heartily about therapy, but she knew deep down he knew he had to do it.

She went out to the kitchen to make Hank breakfast. The men were already up eating cold cereal—while Buck made sandwiches and was pouring coffee in thermos's—he stopped in mid air—when he seen her—Sid whistled—wow they all went. Pleased Dana did a little side step bowing, "Nurse Paine at your service. What can I do for you—enema—pain pills?" A lot of laughter. She made oatmeal for Hank and toast—while that was cooking she wrapped up the rest of the cake for the men's lunch. Buck asked, "If he should go with her." "Oh, Rosa's driving—hell—I still don't know where I'm at besides trying to find a town. Oh, also by the way I have a grocery list for Rosa—ah—how do we pay?" Buck signed a check, when Rosa came in Dana handed it to her. She announced, "Tomorrow I will make breakfast, no therapy tomorrow, today might be a nightmare for him, the first day there is a lot of pain, I hope he's not too mad at me when we get home.

There was a ramp from the kitchen door down to the garage floor. Rosa drove the car out, and then backed in so Hank could get in easier. Everyone hovered around as Dana put his wheelchair in the trunk. Then, "Mr. Hank you grab the top of the door while I swing you in the seat. "You could tell how white his face was as he settled in the car seat. That it hurt. She leaned in looking him in the eye, "Today is the worst day—please believe me." Buck nervous, "Should I go?" "Naw, get to work we'll be fine."

When they got to the clinic Hank had to see the doctor first and then the therapist—so they told Dana to go shopping for an hour.

She asked Rosa to stop by a hardware store first—she turned to Rosa—ah—"Would it make you mad if I buy some tile cleaner and something to clean the bricks on the fireplace?" "Miss Dana you can buy anything you want—I can't keep up with my own house—much less that big house." Happily, Dana marched in a hardware store and asked all kinds of questions for special cleaning supplies for tiles bricks and bathtubs. Dana insisted on paying with her own money.

Rosa and Dana had a blast shopping in the grocery store everyone in there knew Rosa and she introduced Dana all around. The time just flew by.

When they got back to the clinic she hurried to the therapy department. Hank—sweat running down his face—was walking between two bars. The therapist said, "He's doing real good, but maybe extra pain pills and a good long nap for the rest of the day."

Manuel was waiting for them at home Rosa had called him, that Mr. Hank was pretty sore and they might need him. Manuel helped Dana get him in his chair. Hank's weary quiet voice, "Can I get in bed and eat there? I planned on taking you girls out to dinner, but pooped out real fast." "Yes, yes," from an angry Dana, "I don't know why the hell they pushed you so hard you first day. It made me mad. I might have a few things to say to that damn therapist the next time!" Her eyes were just flashing. Hank laughed, "I thought you might be a spit fire after we got to know you. Dana dear, I asked to go the last time." Dana stood him up pulled off his dress pants then put him in bed with an ice pack.

Rosa took leftovers from the fridge and set out a meal and a tray for Hank. Dana started fruit soup ingredients in a big kettle. Manuel stayed to eat.

Dana asked Manuel if he would show her the in and outs of the riding lawn mower and where the gas and oil was kept. At first he was reluctant then said, "Have you ever mowed before? That's kind of a man's job. It's a big mower and I don't know if you can run it. Dana laughed, "Ha, I have news for you Manuel there's not many things I can't do and I CAN run any kind of mower. "Well all right but why today I'll get it done some time." Rosa went, "Yeah right you say that every week. I'll stay with Mr. Hank and Missy you go out there and prove this old poop that women are just as good as men—humphh—."

Dana changed into a black tank top and black bike shorts with cowboy boots on and a huge sweat band on her head. When Rosa and Manuel seen her they covered their mouths trying not to laugh. She said, "Go ahead laugh, snakes can hide in tall grass you know, they're not going to bite me through cowboy boots." Dana peeled potatoes and put a dozen eggs in another kettle and told Rosa they should be cooked in about thirty minutes. She had thawed out a spiral ham from the deep freeze yesterday so she asked Rosa to put that in the oven later. She said, "I will make potato salad tonight.

After Manuel showed her where everything was he stood with his arms crossed watching her back the riding lawn mower out of the garage. He yelled over the noise of the mower, "By God I never seen a woman who knows about machinery, Mr. Hank never even trusted me with his precious mower. Can you run farm machinery too!" "You betcha "She yelled back.

Rosa went in to tell Hank, "Miss Dana's got Manuel all surprised-he thinks all women are just plain dumb when it comes to driving —Ha—I guess she showed him. I'm going to surprise her and try some of this tile cleaner she bought. If it stinks too much let me know?" Hank yawned, "All I want to do is sleep don't worry about me." Rosa started on the hallway she was shocked when it turned out to be white after she wiped up the cleaner. She thought—shit—I always thought this tile was beige. Then she remembered Dana did not have sun screen on, she ran outside and insisted Dana cover every bit of her white skin.

Dana was pleased after a couple of hours to see how nice the yard looked. There were big bushes set in rocks around the log cabin style house. The bottom of the logs was stone or bricks of some kind. There were bushes and rocks along a split rail fence. Wow, she thought this place could be beautiful with some tender loving care.

About 3:30 p.m. a big fancy Lincoln car drove up—a long curly—haired—blonde—got out—little shorts and a halter top—looked like a model or a Hollywood star. On the passenger side another fancy looking lady stepped out. They looked almost like twins, bleached blonde hair—long nails—high heels with shorts—like bright canary birds—Dana thought. Dana realized they were shocked at her appearance, well so what, she shut the mower off and clunked over to them in her cowboy boots. She could tell they were trying hard not to laugh. They introduced themselves as neighbors from up the road. They had heard there was a new nurse, but—ah—they didn't expect her to be mowing. Dana laughed, "It's time for a break come in Rosa made lemonade and I need a break from the sun—Holy cow—I didn't think I would get so hot."

They followed her in the house and asked, "If they could see Hank?" Dana peeked in his room—Rosa was sound asleep in the recliner beside Hanks bed and he was snoring. Dana whispering, "I guess we had better let them sleep, let's have a cold drink and a cookie." "Did Rosa make them?" "No store bought, so you know about the cookies huh?" They introduced themselves as Connie and Billie West. They said, "Both their husbands had passed away and they had come back to their Aunt's ranch to live a year ago. They said it took two years for a new house to be built for them and their Aunt and was enjoying living in the sticks. They had their own airplane and a runway that Buck used too—they had their own cattle—registered Angus cattle they were very proud of raising—well with lots of men to help. Dana thought privately looking at their perfect makeup and manicured nails; I'll bet you have lots of help. They were all three sitting around the huge round oak table, Dana asking them all about their ranch when she noticed Rosa had cleaned some of the tile, surprised she said, "Oh, I didn't want Rosa to do that but is sure is pretty, look how white it is, my goodness." Billie said, "Well, Liz kept this house just perfect, it was really nice twenty years ago—I don't know why Buck insists on keeping that ugly Mediterranean furniture with white carpet it's so old fashioned. Everything is brown and beige now."

Dana shocked, "I love the living room—white carpet—red velvet curtains—of course it's going to need a good cleaning and I plan on doing that soon." Horrified the newcomers looked at her, "Well each to their own I guess." Dana took a better look at the huge living room right off the dining room—a white brick fireplace covered one wall—a big screen TV on one side—three big brown recliners was facing the TV, but the huge couch was flowered red and white. Dana thought it was a charming, but dirty room.

About this time Rosa came out walked right by them to the utility room—not a word. Dana said, "Rosa that tile is beautiful. Did that stuff smell? Come have lunch with us." "No, I'm busy!!" Dana uncomfortable looked at the two women and shrugged her shoulders; she couldn't help noticing they didn't speak to Rosa either. Both women got up Billie said, "Tell Hank hello and tell Buck I'll see him Saturday night at the dance in town. Oh, and we stopped to invite you all to a bar-b-que at our house Sunday night. It's too bad if you can't come and leave Hank, so see if you can get him to come." Dana said, "sure that sounds fun.' Dana followed them out to their car. As they drove off they waved goodbye.

She went back to the house to make the potato salad and to check on Hank who was feeling better and was glad to take an extra pain pill.

When Rosa came out of the laundry room she made a cross with her fingers on each hand, then she held her nose and said, "Those two are trouble with a capital T—ever since they moved here with all their money—well that Billie thinks she owns Mr. Buck. He's just like all men, looking at that body instead of her head." Dana really laughed now, 'She pretty well laid that out to me, like I'm a threat—oh well who cares—she looks like pretty hot stuff." Rosa went Humph, "Outside pretty—inside evil. We should spray this house; they bring the devil with them where ever they go—mark my words Miss Dana!" Dana amused went back to her mowing.

CHAPTER 9

MARIA LOPEZ WAS STANDING by her kitchen window watching the sunrise still in her robe she knew it was too early to be up, but could not sleep. Something was heavy on her heart, she felt afraid shaky inside. Lupe came out to the kitchen, "Ma what are you doing up. I couldn't sleep I heard you up moving around. What's the matter are you sick?" Maria turned slowly looking at him, "No, I'm not sick I have bad feeling in my heart—she held her hand over her heart." Lupe terrified, "You mean a heart attack?" "No—a bad feeling of something bad going to happen." He sighed, "You mean one of your premonitions? What are you worried about Senna? Or money? I have quite a bit of goat milk to sell today; the sister at the hospital says they can use more.

You were asleep last night when I came home. Mr. Argo invited me over.—He is lonely with Carlotta gone—he wants to sell me two more nanny goats so I will have more milk to sell—he will accept monthly payments—I told him I would do this." Maria said, "Lupe, you are good son. Ever since your father was killed I have tried to care for you and Senna the best way I knew how. The money from the hotel really helps—no, that's not my bad feeling. It's something else. I'm so worried about Senna. She has not wrote us and there has been no money sent to me at the hotel, like that Mr. Damon promised. Yes, this is not like Senna to forget us. I wish I would have tried harder to keep her here, but she is twenty-one and very —ah—headstrong—I know she wants a better life than Mexico can give her. I just wish she would write. Oh, my look at the time, I must hurry now—the new manager seems to be kind, but it would not be wise to be late. Lupe, why don't you stop in after you deliver the milk, we will have my lunch break to visit.—Since Mr. Tate came we even get cookies and other ladies children stop—yes, do this—okay?" Lupe said, "Hey is there a new cute girl working there? What is her name?" Maria puzzled, "How you know new girl come? You hear this or did you see her?" Lupe blushed, "I met her one night at the pizza place, she knows you. She told me she worked with you and you were nice lady. She said, "You are very pretty for your age, with such nice skin, and you have kept your body in good shape, not like others here, who get fat like pigs and no teeth." Maria was dressing now and yelled from the bedroom, "Always compliment your future relative in case she want to marry my Lupe. She is good worker and her name is Ann. More reason for you to stop in for lunch, huh?"

Maria felt better as she got in her old car for work—She still felt scared for some reason, but was happy to go to work and get her mind off things at home. She was a good housekeeper, she even made tips from some of the regular customers, and she vacuumed, dusted and was really fussy about the bathrooms.

The girls were all glad to see Maria when she got to work—everyone was setting up their cleaning carts-chattering—like they did every morning. Nika who had worked a long time with Maria, asked her. "What's wrong . . . . you don't look right?" Maria holding her hand over her heart, "I wish I knew and no, I'm not having a heart attack . . . it's something else I feel heavy and slow and scared . . . I can't explain . . . I tried to tell Lupe this morning . . . He was nice about it, but I think he was just humoring me. He thinks my premonitions are stupid!"

All the girls giggled at the mention of Lupe. Maria proud for a minute thought, my Lupe is a handsome boy. I hope he is being careful with all these girls after him. I know he goes to Geron's Bar on Friday and Saturday nights, that's where he probably meets all of them.

Maria smiling, "Forgive a foolish old woman, maybe I'm depressed or something like that. Let's get to work." Everyone laughed, "No matter if the world was going to end tomorrow you would still think we had to clean these rich people's rooms. Maria, do you ever do anything for fun? "Maria waved her arms enough, "Get to work you lazy girls. Sometime I will fool all of you and come to the Geron place one night and show you an old lady can still party . . . Ha" Then she told them, "Lupe is coming to have break with us today." Now the girls started looking at their hair and makeup.

Maria hurried off with her cart smiling to herself. Well, that really perked the girls up. I wish on the inside I felt better. I hate to waste a day feeling bad . . . life is too short.

At lunch time Maria called all the girls on her walkie talkie. "Time for lunch." Everyone gathered in the employee lounge, laughing, telling stories of what they found in the rooms this morning. One said, "You know that old couple that stayed three days, well guess what? There was thong underwear under the bed, his and hers?" The peals of laughing women directed Lupe to the right room.

As he walked in Maria thought, "Oh my, he looks like a movie star . . . my handsome son. I just hope he has sense enough to keep his man toy in his pants. These girls are just gaga about him, they would do anything to trap him into marriage. We barely make a living now, I don't know what we would do with another mouth to feed and our little house, Oh Dear!" Maria still with a feeling of dread in her heart tried to be happy. She loved all her co-workers like they were her children, but did not need any more trouble in her life.

Mr. Tate came into the room and said, "Maria, you have an emergency phone call in the office. He wouldn't tell me what he wanted, it's a man that's all I know!" Maria flustered hurried to the office; she knew management frowned upon personal phone calls and she loved working for Mr. Tate. He was the best boss she had ever had. She picked up the phone, "Maria Lopez here, the voice on the phone was Damon, and he said "I have some bad news for you and I don't know how to tell you this—it's bad. Is there someone with you there?" Maria had the secretary go get Lupe from the break room.

She said, "Tell me Lupe is here with me now." Damon sounding so sorrowful, "Senna is gone—she drowned on a family picnic we were having with some of the girls—we have not found her body yet, but still searching. She got caught in a whirlpool in a river and was gone before we could save her!!" Maria fell to the floor in a dead faint; Lupe grabbed the phone, "What are you telling us? You took my sister swimming? Senna hates water. How could this happen? Is Carlotta there let me talk to her? Was she there when this happened? All the staff was bending over Maria with wet washcloths and crying. "Senna is dead?" Their eyes were huge all shocked. Nika said, "Maria knew something was wrong, she has felt troubled all day. It's like she sensed big trouble, what can we do to help?"

Lupe hung up the phone holding his head in his hands, body shaking, This Damon that got Senna the job in America—Well, he says Senna drowned at a picnic and Carlotta ran off to marry some old man she met there. I just can't get my mind around all this." Maria tears running down her face said, 'Lupe take me home—now." Lupe asked Nika, "If she could drive a stick shift pickup." "Yes." "Then can you drive my pickup out to the farm when you get done working. I will bring you back later after we get this sorted out." Someone needs to call Father John so he can come out and tell Mr. Argo about Carlotta."

Mr. Tate said, "I will go to Father John and tell him all that we know at this time. Did this Damon give you a number to call? Yes, but I don't trust him. He acts nice, but I don't think he is, I never wanted Senna to do this foolish thing. He told me he is going to send Ma a check and he will stop in next time he is in the area."

If Lupe could have seen the smile on Damon's face when he hung up the phone, Lupe would have killed him with his bare hands.

CHAPTER 10

Father John was out of bed by 7:00, his usual routine. First, prayers for all his poor parishioners. He wished he could help all of them, but could only give comfort through the word of God. That at least God cared and truly they would not go hungry, but no luxuries in their lives. Some as always had more than others. Why? Father John could not second guess God, and what he wanted to do. Father John finished his prayer time.

He heard rather than seen Myra come in to the kitchen. She was a very large Mexican woman, who could move faster than most people he knew. How she could cook, clean house and watch over him, like a hawk plus take care of her own family. Ten children, many now grown, well she was a human dynamo and bossy as hell.

Myra called out to him, "I have breakfast ready." He knew it would be oatmeal and toast with Myra's wonderful homemade jelly. He said, "Eat with me Myra. I get tired of eating alone. Tell me what's going on in the neighborhood. At least have a cup of coffee." Myra joined him at the table. They talked about her children and who was having a baby and who was getting married. He once again told her how much he appreciated all she did for him. He said, "It's cooler out I'm going to work in the garden for a while."

Father John put his hat on and went out to the garden. He faithfully kept a huge vegetable garden, giving most of it away. It was the only extra help he could give to the people of the church. Myra called to Father John, "Come eat." He answered, "One more minute. I'm about done."

MYRA HEARD THE DOOR bell ring and hurried to the house. She was shocked to see Mr. Tate standing at the door, "Well, my goodness, come in. We have heard such good things about you! Sorry sir, this is a small town, we all know who's new in town." Mr. Tate, "Thank you, my family and I are Catholic and we will be coming to your church, but we have been so busy getting settled in our new home. Your name?' Myra flustered, "I'm Father John's housekeeper, my name is Myra and I am pleased to meet you. Father is out in the garden I will take you out there."

They walked together around the house and found Father with his white hair standing on end and dripping with sweat. Myra pointing her finger at him, "Where's your hat? Old man, you are going to just drop dead sometime out here and I can't watch you all the time. This here is Mr. Tate, you know, the new man that owns the hotel?" Father John stood up bright blue eyes twinkling, "Do you let your employees talk to you like this? Hello, the marvelous Mr. Tate, your employees says you are the best boss."

Mr. Tate uncomfortable, "I have some bad news for you—ah—Maria Lopez got a phone call at work during lunch time that her daughter Senna had drowned and was dead. They can't find her body yet and Mr. Argo's daughter Carlotta ran off with an old American man. Lupe asked if you could come out their way and tell Mr. Argo and comfort Maria."

Father John shook his fist at the sky and yelled, "WHY? Tell me why? He turned to Mr. Tate embarrassed. "I'm sorry. Even I can have anger at God, he forgives you know, I get so mad for my people they already suffer enough. Tears in his eyes, poor Maria, Senna just wanted a better life." Myra started wailing her apron flung over her face, "Noooooooo!" Let's go inside and have a glass of lemonade."

They all three sat at the table in the parsonage trying to make sense of all this. Father John had washed his hands, but dirt still clung to his clothes. He said, "I will shower and go right out to Lopez's and see Argo. Oh my, this is so awful." Mr. Tate left with a heavy heart thinking what a fine old man Father John was and he certainly did not envy him his awful job breaking news to people with burdens enough.

CHAPTER 11

DANA MOWED ANOTHER HOUR and then cleaned and put the mower away. She hurried to make the potato salad. Mr. Hank had requested banana crème pie. She didn't tell him she had bought ready to bake pie crust.

As she was cooking Rosa and the children came in. Mikala shyly handed Dana a special envelope to open. Inside Dana found an engraved invitation to her "Quinceanera" Friday night the next week. Dana hand over her heart, "Oh Mikala, I would love to come, believe it or not, I have attended something like this in South Dakota, at the Catholic church for a daughter of a woman I worked with, it was beautiful, I feel dumb, but I didn't know what it was called." Mikala, explained it was a coming out party for girls who was fourteen. Then she asked Dana if they could pick pecans today. I see you mowed under the trees. I would like to bag some and sell at the Farmers Market. Mr. Hank used to like shelling them too."

Rosa said, "Oh Mikala is determined to earn sixty more dollars for a special dress, she is supposed to wear her grandmother's dress—sniffing—but of course, that's not good enough for her. Manuel says we are only spending fifty dollars for a different dress. It already costs for the food. Both grandmothers' are making special treats for the dance and party afterwards. And hands on her hips pointing at Mikala, we did buy those fancy high heels you wanted!" Mikala hung her head, not sure what to say or do. Dana thought a minute, "If I'm not sticking my nose in where it doesn't belong, can I ask? Mikala could you help me for about five hours on this Saturday? I well-ah—if I'm not being pushy, ah, I would like to do the living room. I found a rug shampoo machine in the closet. Hank says, "Martha and Buck are taking him to a funeral that day." So I thought —well—I want to clean the bricks on the fireplace—shampoo the white carpet—do the curtains and put some silk flowers around on the end tables—I don't know—maybe bring those fancy red chairs in from the office—hastily she went on—I know the men like their big recliners. I wouldn't change them."

Mikala looking toward Rosa, "Ma, please can I?" Rosa eyes flashing for a quick minute, "I know you think things are to plain here, Miss Dana, but Hank and I put Miss Liz's fancy stuff upstairs in a room, he said he didn't know how to clean all that junk and I do not have time!!" "Oh!" Dana apologized, "I'm sorry Rosa—please, I have lots of time while he sleeps and I just think that room could be so pretty—if it makes you mad I won't do it. I think you can tell I like doing housework and love being outside. Please don't be mad at me!'

Rosa had to laugh, "You are a crazy woman. Do you always talk, talk, talk and work, work, work?" "Yeah", Dana said, "I admit it I'm a little hyperactive—well maybe a lot!" Rosa snorted waving her arms, "I think it would be nice to have Miss Liz's stuff out again, yes, clapping her hands. Mikala and I will both help. As to the fancy dress we will see!" Mikala jumping up and down, "Dad said I could have fifty dollars, so if I sell some pecans and work for Miss Dana—please, please—convince Dad I can buy the dress!" Dana said, "I will give you fifty dollars to help me—will that be all right, Rosa?" Rosa smiling, "We will see!"

Hank called out then, "I'm ready to get up, who the hell could sleep with all that yammering going on. Yes, Dana you can fix up the house and I Will GIVE THE KID $50, now let's get those pecans shelled out," Everyone moved it out. The children took a tarp and raked pecans on it. Dana helped Hank up. Worried he might be hurting from his therapy, but to both of their surprise, he seemed more limber. Dana got him in his wheelchair and pushed him out to the front porch.

The kids had two five gallon pails of pecans picked already. Josh ran home to get bags. Hank told Dana where to find nut crackers. Dana and the kids laid the tarps under the trees so the next day it would be much easier than raking them up.

When the men came in from the field, they found Hank drinking beer, Dana, wine. Rosa and the kids sodas. They were surprised to find they had two garbage bags of pecan shells. The first thing Buck said, "Where's the famous cowboy boots?" Everyone looked at him. Then Dana threw her arms in the air, "I only need the boots when I mow. I'm not taking a chance on running into or over a snake with bare ankles!" "Well," he said, "This place really looks nice. Dad, did you tell her she had to mow?" "No," Dana said horrified, No, I love to mow." Mikala answered Buck serious, "Miss Dana has something wrong with her, hyperactive or something, well, looking around her at everybody laughing. What's so funny?"

"Dana stopped laughing and stopped short, "How do you know about the —boots?" "Ha," "Rosa said making a cross with her fingers. "Those two devils were here, they came out to the field . . . didn't they? Manny you had better have stayed away from them, I mean it!" One more family laugh, Buck, "I almost forgot —the devils—looking at Rosa—have changed the time for the barbeque to Sunday night."

After supper everyone said, "Dana that was the best meal. You are a good cook, we are all getting spoiled. I hope you plan on staying????"

The next morning Dana was up early to help Buck make sandwiches, she told him, "When Hank feels better we will bring lunch out to the field. Can we get through with the car?" "Dad would like that and yes you can come out with the car to some of the fields, he knows which ones are easiest to get to."

Buck stopped filling his thermos and said, "Ah—Dana why don't you call Martha to have supper with us tonight and then stay with Dad while you and I take a copula of horses out so you can see more of the ranch?" Dana out and out moaned, "Oh, God —Buck, I have not rode a horse for twenty years, I'm not that crazy about riding!" Buck mused, "Well, that's funny. I see every time you're out in the yard the horses run up to the fence. What's that about?" Dana looked sheepish, "I love horses. I just don't like to ride them—ah—I kind of cleaned some old apples and carrots from the fridge and treated the horses. Well, what the hell!—Find me a nice quiet girl horse and I would love to see what's over the hill from the ranch." Tonight he said, "Tonight we will see the most beautiful sunset you have ever seen I promise."

After breakfast Hank and Dana sat on the porch, with their coffee, cigar, cigarette for Dana. He started talking about his life with his wonderful wife. He said, "It about killed Liz when Buck's wife left and took their little girl and Sid with her.

Then, of course, Sid came home, Liz had them move out here and she raised Sid. Girl if you want to bring some of Liz's doo dads down from upstairs, you sure can. Rosa was afraid she would break something and I didn't care one way or the other. My daughter brought some things down and put on the mantel. Rosa had a fit, "Don't expect me to dust them." she said!" Dana, you are just what we need here to put some life back in this place. The yard looks nice and your cheerful disposition is—well—special." Dana pleased said, "Thank you. I like being busy. Rosa says I'm a crazy lady, but I feel good when my body is moving.

My first husband told me I made him nuts with all the cleaning, vacuuming, and changing furniture around in the house. His next complaint was I was constantly outside in the summer. In his mind, it was not necessary to keep everything mowed and all the barns clean. He finally left the girls and I on the farm with all the milk cows and bought a camper and took off traveling all over. He still sends the girls money on their birthdays and Christmas. They didn't seem too upset when he left, and quite frankly, I was glad to see him gone.

I sold the cows during the government buy out for dairy cattle and bought stock cows. We managed for about a year with my working full time and keeping up the farm, then I met my second husband, who the girls really consider their father. He was so good to all of us. We were married five years when he got pancreatic cancer and was gone in three months. That was a terrible time for us, I had to sell the farm, to pay off debts and buy a house in town.

The winters are just so bad in South Dakota, I could not keep up with the animals and the snow removal. We all hated it in town, but had to accept what we had. That's why I love it here all ready because it's so peaceful, no traffic, no neighbors watching or stopping in to have coffee, because they had nothing else to do. Although, I did enjoy your neighbor ladies stopping in the other day, even though Rosa says their witches, I got a big kick out of them."

"Well, Mr. Hank," I think it's time we get you off to bed, Rosa's coming over after lunch for her afternoon nap in your chair and I'm going to use the push mower. Manuel finally—well not quite sure yet—if I am to be trusted with a mower. He has explained the push mower in detail to me. I didn't tell him I have been running a push mower since I was twelve years old. I respectably listened to his dire warnings—about cutting off my fingers or my feet or a rock hitting me in the head and knocking me out!" Hank said, "Don't make me laugh like this, he was just roaring. Girl, I still have pain, you are so damn funny."

After settling Hank for a rest, Dana started a batch of cookies and still worked on the huge mound of laundry. She worked on more of the tile in the kitchen while the cookies baked. She then started in on the bathroom everything in the bathroom was covered in soap scum. The toilet and tub had a dirty ring about two inches wide all around the fixtures.

She was busy until almost lunch time, when her daughter Lucy called, she stopped for coffee and a long chat. Lucy did not have classes this morning, she wanted Dana to describe all the people and what the ranch looked like.

"Well," Dana said, "Rosa and Manuel are the hired couple they live in a house behind the ranch house. They have three of the cutest kids. Rosa is a pretty Mexican woman short, but thin, Manuel is stocky and very good looking, they have been really nice to me. Their daughter is having her Latino coming out next week, you know like Lehto's. We went to there at the Catholic church. Mr. Hank looks like John Wayne—Buck looks like—oh what's his name?—you know the Sunday night movie guy—Stony Point or something like that—I can't remember his name.!" Lucy squealed, "You mean Tom Selleck? Wow, mom he is a cool dude, even if he is pretty grey now. Does this Buck have black hair and mustache like Selleck used to have?

"Yeah," from Dana, "his son Sid looks like Tom Cruise. They all have black hair and blue eyes except of course, Hank has white thick hair, but bright blue eyes. Then there is another hired man named Pete, He looks like those Argentine gauchos or cowboys, he has dark eyes kind of like a hawk, hooded. They all seem like decent men. I think this Sid is kinda a ladies' man and Buck seems to have something going with a neighbor lady here, she came to visit me with a little kind of threat to leave him alone. I had to laugh she looks like a lady of the night, all painted up, Hank seems to have a lady friend named Martha and she is just a cute little old lady, so sweet and seems to have just a friendship with Hank."

Lucy said, "Mom, you're having fun. I can tell." Dana, "I sure am, I love it here so far. There is lots of stuff to do like yard work and house cleaning and laundry—and my favorite cooking for people who appreciate it.

Now tell me about everybody at home. What's been going on there?" Lucy talked a few more minutes and then asked if Dana needed anything. "At first Dana said, No, then she happened to think about Mikala's party. Lucy, would you send my long red dress with the slit up the side and the heels to match, oh, and my rhinestone jewelry. You know what, send my long black dress too. Send it all UPS so I get it soon, I will need to see if it needs cleaning."

When they hung up the phone it was time to fix Hank's lunch. He wanted something light like a sandwich in bed, if he could, he asked, "What's for supper?" Dana said, "I found some frozen roasts in the freezer, so I have them with carrots, onions, and potatoes in two crock pots. If I can buy two cups of pecans from the kids, we will have pies.'

Rosa came and had a sandwich with them. Then her and Hank watched a T.V. show while Dana got on her famous cowboy boots, shorts and her big hat so she could push mow around the bushes and get closer to the rock around the bushes by the house, then she was going to use the weed eater to clean up under the fence. She told Bo dog, "You stay with me in case we have unwanted creepy crawlers in the yard." Bo stretched, yawned and moved under a tree. Dana said to him,"—some protector you are—huh—Stay with me. If I can stand the heat so can you!"

When the kids got home from school they ran over to watch Dana crawl around on her hands and knees cleaning weeds from the rocks. They said, "We have to go to church tonight so we can't do pecans." Dana said, "It's time for a break lets go have cookies and milk, your Mom and Hank are probably awake now."

Rosa came out from Hank's room and said, "Why didn't you wake me up before?" I could have helped you." Dana laughed, "My dear, I think you needed to rest. Kids, can I buy some pecans from you so I can bake pies for tonight? Martha's coming over I want to have something special for her."

Rosa said to the kids, "Martha's coming to stay with Hank so Buck can take Miss Dana on a moonlight horseback ride." The kids all went, "Ooooo, Is he your boyfriend now?" Dana rolled her eyes and laughed, "I doubt if Buck could be very interested in me when he has Miss Billie right up the road. She looks to be a little more the romantic type than me. I think he's just trying to be nice and I told him I'm not a very good rider. I like messing with horses as long as I don't have to ride them. He says the view up on the hill is something to see, so I hope I don't fall off the damn horse. Sorry kids, excuse the language." The kids were laughing so hard they were about lying on the floor. Mikala said, "What if he kisses you?" "Holy Cow," Dana fanning her hand in front of her face, "Well now, this night could turn out to be the most excitement I've had in a long time. I hate to disappoint you little darlings, but I think I'm too old for such nonsense."

Supper turned out to be a hit with everyone. Dana was tired, but so pleased about all the compliments about the house getting cleaned up and the yard looked like somebody lived there again and best of all how much they liked her cooking.

After supper Buck brought two horses, saddled, up to the house, "Ready to go Nurse Paine?" Dana patted her horse, "Now let's get this straight, what's her name, (Queenie), okay girl, be good to me, I bet I'm older than you and I might just fall off, so don't run off or step on me, oh, and no trying to knock me off on a tree branch and please do not step in a hole. Are we on the same page here?" To Dana's delight Queenie shook her head up and down. Dana carefully pulled herself up in the saddle, "God, I didn't think I could swing my legs over a horse anymore, well by golly, let's ride off into the sunset—yahoo!" Buck laughed.

For a while they didn't talk until Dana got used to riding, then she asked Buck about his wife. He said, "I met her at a 4-H convention in D.C., love at first sight. We kept calling each other and then she came to visit and I went to her folks, anyway after a year or so, we decided to get married. We bought a house in town because she knew she couldn't live out here. It was like a foreign land to her, she hated the isolation out here. After a few years she got depressed in town, not enough social events, and she did not like housework or cooking. Finally, she took the kids and moved back to Florida by her folks. She has a store there and remarried an attorney. Sid, of course hated Florida, so he came home. He still keeps the house in town, but rarely goes there."

When they got to the top of the hill behind the ranch, Dana stopped dead still holding tight to Queenie's reins. In awe, she said, "Oh my God, I had no idea, this is just so beautiful, oh my God, the sunset is every color of the rainbow! I can see for miles. Oh, thank you Buck for talking me into this. I was so tired after supper I thought all I want to do is go to bed." Buck helped her down from her horse, they sat on a rock and watched the moon come up. It seemed the most natural thing in the world when he reached out and held her hand. Dana thought, what a nice man, this is just what I needed, out loud she said, "I know what God meant when he said, "You will lie down in green pastures and I will restore your soul, I feel restored. Buck, do you believe in God?" Buck thought for a minute, "A rancher has to believe in the Almighty, I have to ask for help ten times a day."

They rode home talking quietly about the problems each of them had lived through. When they got to the barn, Dana took her own saddle off and found a box of sugar cubes in the tack room of the barn. She gave Queenie two and then hugged the horse.

Thursday morning came too early for Dana it was all she could do to drag herself out of bed, but it was therapy day and Hank actually wanted to go. Dana hurried around getting Hank dressed and insisted he take an extra pain pil., It would help with the strenuous therapy. Buck made breakfast and waited to help Dana get Hank in the car. Buck looked at Dana in her professional uniform and thought—my goodness—she is a beautiful woman, I wonder if she knows?

Once again Rosa drove with Dana's grocery list along, she was going to do the shopping today while Dana stayed with Hank to observe how he was doing. Hank was determined to go to a funeral on Saturday and wanted to be able to help himself get in the wheelchair. Dana was impressed with the therapist and how she handled Hank.

When they were done Hank said, "Today, Miss Dana we are going out to eat." Dana laughed, "Well maybe we had better wait until there's more help to get you in and out of the wheelchair . . . . okay?" "No," he said, "What we will do is you push this damn chair down the street here to the Sunbird lounge. Call Rosa and tell her to meet us there." Dana, "Wow, you really feel like going out? This is a big improvement from the first day." Hank said, "You were right the pain pills made a hell of a difference. I just hope I don't get addicted or something, like all those crazy movie stars I see on T.V.!"

It was a gorgeous day and Dana felt so happy to see him coming along so fast. She called Rosa, who was as surprised as Dana, to think he was feeling good after a rather long therapy session. Dana and Hank rolled down the street to what looked like a bar to Dana.

The inside was dark after the bright sunshine outside, but Dana thought now this is my kind of place, red checkered tablecloths with baskets of white mum flowers on each table and clean, shiny floors. When they started for a table all kinds of people came over to shake Hank's hand. They all said, "We thought you died, you old fart, died and never told any of us goodbye, and what kind of friend are you anyway? Dana started to laugh, when Hank introduced her as Nurse Paine, "And that's just what she is, a pain in the ass, but she said she would get me moving again and by golly she knew what she was talking about, I can't walk yet, but at least I can stand the pain now, so I feel good enough to put up with all the bullshit going on in this place, damn I forgot my hip boots. I'll bet it's thick in here today." By now everyone roared and clapped for Hank. Dana laughed until the tears ran down her face.

They got settled at a table and Rosa showed up. She was so tickled to see Hank getting back to his normal ornery self, she self consciously gave Hank a hug. Hank surprised, "Well now, you keep that up and I might start chasing you around the house." Rosa blushed, but Dana could tell she was pleased. The waitress came to take their order Dana said, "I will have a hamburger with the homemade fries. Are they the thick ones?"

Before the waitress could answer there was a flurry of interest from people, especially men, Connie and Billie West entered the lounge helping their Aunt Eva with her walker. They came right over to Hank and got a chair for Eva to sit by Hank, then Billie kissed him on top of his head and said, "Oh, how good it is to see you up and about. We saw the car outside. Connie, sit beside Dana and I will sit by Hank." Rosa sitting next to Dana fluffed up, she reminded Dana of a bantam chicken hen if you touched her chicks, they would take on anything or anybody that posed a threat, in their minds. Billie said to Dana, "Where's the cowboy boots. Boy, you sure look different today, you clean up good!" "Well, thank you," Dana said. "You look REALLY GOOD TOO, how do you keep your hair and nails like that. You are a beautiful woman!"

The waitress was still waiting so everyone ordered, of course, Connie and Billie ordered salads and then looked shocked as Dana ordered her big meal. Dana amused thought they really are some hot looking chicks in their short, short, shorts and just a touch of brown belly under their skimpy tops. Rosa said to the waitress, "We can't stay long Mr. Hank gets to tired, so could you kind of hurry our order."

Billie said to Dana, "I heard you went out riding with Buck last night. Did you enjoy that?" Dana puzzled, "Yes it's the first time I have got to see what was above the hill from the ranch. I'm a terrible horse rider so we didn't go very far." Dana watched Billie's face as she talked she thought, holy shit, if looks could kill, I would be dead. The conversation turned to more about the barbeque on Sunday night at the West's. Hank told them, "He was not coming, but Dana should meet some of the other neighbors, so he insisted she would come." Dana said, "I plan on coming for just a little while, Martha's coming to watch a movie with Hank, so I am looking forward to seeing your beautiful house and I hear your landscaping is really unique."

Hank did start looking tired after a while. Dana said, 'Goodbye to the new people she had met and then two of the men from the lounge came with them to the car to help Hank in and put his wheelchair in the trunk. Dana thanked them and they said don't thank us, it's you that got him moving again.

On the way home Hank said, "Rosa, stop at that pizza place before we leave town. We are having pizza tonight and our nurse is going to take an afternoon nap and sit down and rest for the rest of this day, Dana, that's an order!" Dana laughed, "You are right. I think I do need a nap and no cooking sounds good to me."

Manuel was waiting for them when they got home to help with Hank, Rosa brought him take out from the lounge. She told Manuel, 'That Billie came in while we were at the Sunbird and was nasty to Miss Dana, Dana so innocent she doesn't get it. I could just knock that woman on her ass, Billie, I mean, she started in on Dana about Buck taking her out riding last night!' Manuel and Dana laughed, Dana said, "Oh, I get it all right Rosa, but I think it is hilarious!!"

After Hank was back in bed with some more pain medication, Dana laid back in the recliner in his room.

Then Dana said, Oh, my God I forgot to call that little girl from the plane, I was telling you about. Oh my, I'll use my cell phone and call her right now." Lucia answered on the first ring, "Thank you God, when I seen your name on my caller I.D., Josh keeps asking about you.

I just got out of the hospital yesterday I did have broken ribs. I feel like a new person, except well—aha—Richard is trying all kinds of stuff threats about custody of the kids and now Dad is afraid he will hire one of those—oh you know—those people that steal kids away and hide them in another country with their Dad.

Dad got the kids settled in a Catholic private school here and he takes them and brings them home every day. Actually Dad is afraid for any of us to go anyplace without all of us together. Could you come visit us or—ah—could we come there to see you. Is it far from El Paso?" "Just a minute," Dana said, holding her hand over the phone. "She asked Hank, "If they could all come here maybe for Sunday dinner, Dana would make it." Hank said, "You tell them they're welcome here any time. Why don't you have them meet us at the Sunbird Lounge—oh say—about 1:00 Sunday and then they can follow us out to the ranch and Sid can get the Welch ponies out for the kids to ride. Are they about Rosa's kid's age?"

"Yes, thank you Hank." Dana back on the phone, "Lucia, Hank says your always welcome here. He wants to know if you could meet us for Sunday dinner at the Sunbird Lounge in Sunbird for dinner about 1:00 and then follow us out to the ranch. He will ask his grandson to catch the little horses so the kid's can ride and the couple that work here have children about the same age as yours. Oh, I hope you can come that will be so much fun." Lucia started crying. Dana shocked asked, "What's the matter—ah—maybe your folks won't come? They are invited too I hope you understood that."

Lucia said, "I was so afraid to call you, I thought maybe you wouldn't want anything to do with us after that mess on the plane and then the way Dad acted, Oh, Dana we want to see you so bad. I am sure Dad will bring us and I'm sure he knows where Sunbird is. I know he knows the Boldt family you're working for, and he says their real good people. I'll call you tonight for sure, but I think we can come."

Dana breathed a sigh of relief curled up in the chair and was dead to the world in a few minutes.

CHAPTER 12

MR. ARGO WAS DRIVING by the Lopez farm when he saw Lupe with his arms around Maria leading her into the house. He slammed on his brakes and turned in beside Maria's car. Jumping out he said, "What's wrong? Are you sick Maria?" Lupe said, "Come in Arty—aha—we have some bad news!" Maria tears running down her red swollen face from crying choked out, "Senna's dead, Senna's dead!" Mr. Argo, "What are you saying, what do you mean Senna's dead."

Lupe helped Maria to her chair in the living room and then said, "Ma will tell you all about it I'm going to make some coffee, please ma quit crying so hard, I'm afraid you will have a heart attack or something . . . please!" Artie sat on a chair across from Maria, "This is not the time to ask I know but, can you tell me, is Carlotta all right? She's all I have left in this world I didn't want her to go to America but, she wanted so much to leave here. I get so scared for her and I get so lonely since my wife died. It helps that Lupe comes almost every day, I don't know what I would do without him!"

Maria held her hand out to Mr. Argo and said," That man who took our girls away with their big dreams called me at work today and said that Senna had went on a picnic and went in the water and drowned. He then told me that Carlotta had run off with a rich old man." Mr. Argo's face turned white, "No, No, this can't be true. Carlotta would not go away without telling me, I have a phone, no, this is not true. Senna is afraid of water, why would she go swimming? No, this does not sound right." Maria stunned, "I agree this does not sound right. I have never trusted that man. Maybe we had best call Captain Luis. This Damon told me they could not find Senna's body yet." Maria almost hysterical, "Oh, why did I not stop her? Why, why, did she want to leave, we have a good life here even though we are poor.

"Mr. Argo to both their shock fell to his knees in front of Maria's chair and pulled her into his lap as they both sobbed now. Lupe did not know what to do; he kept running his hands through his hair and pacing back and forth in the kitchen. Finally he sat by the table with his head down and simply cried his heart out. He heard a car approaching dried his tears and went to the door, standing there was Nika's mother with her arms full of food. She was a tired out old lady from all the children she raised, her husband was not able to work, so the family depended on her and Nika to keep things going. Lupe was never so glad to see anyone in his life, seeing her already bustling about with coffee and cutting off chunks of homemade bread with goat cheese she had made. She didn't say a word just went to Maria and took her hand, crossed herself, and made both Artie and Maria take a cup of coffee.

Nika was carefully driving Lupe's truck out to the Lopez farm. She had a lot of thoughts going around in her head. She had loved Lupe since they were in school together as little kids, but she did not want Lupe to know. All the girls in town were gaga about him and all of them were just sure he was in love with them.

She loved coming to Maria's house it was so nice compared to how Nika's folks home, they lived at the edge of town in a house more like a shack with five kids, Nika's Mom made quilts and homemade sewing to sell to the tourists in town. She was sure her mother could make a lot more money if she could take her beautiful things to America, but she always told her kids, we have good friends, enough to eat and our place is paid for and best of all we have a good church, even if our house is a mess.

Nika had rented a one room apartment close to her work with her mother's blessing, not much privacy when there are five kids and one bedroom. Nika had painted her apartment a light blue and hung a curtain all around her single bed so it would look like a bedroom; in fact most people thought it was an extra room. She had found a couch and chair at a second hand store and her and her mother went twice a year to the big city and bought material for her Mom's sewing, there they had found some bright blue and pink flowered material they used to make slip covers for Nika's furniture. She had a hot plate and shared a community refrigerator and bathroom with four other apartments. She was so proud of her apartment, her Mom had also found a rug from an auction that sat in the middle of the room, bright blue, with white fringe around the edge.

Driving into Maria's yard she thought again how nice Maria had fixed things up. She had put rocks around the front of the house so people could not drive right up to the door. Nika thought about Maria's house often, it was something she wanted someday. Maria had wallpapered the kitchen with chicken wallpaper; there were bright colored curtains at all the windows. When the hotel was buying some new furnishing, they gave Maria a nice couch and chair set with end tables to match. Maria and Senna had painted flowers and green leaves all over one wall that looked just like a big painting.

At the thought of Senna Nika got tears in her eyes again. She thought God all Senna wanted was a better life, not that I agreed with her because I love it here, but Senna shouldn't have to die for want of a better life, that's just not right.

Lupe come running out to the truck, "Nika I need you, I can't go to pieces in front of Ma, that just makes things worse." He grabbed Nika in a bear hug, sobbing, she led him over to a lawn chair and then drug one over for herself, she reached out and held both his hands, while he cried his heart out, she remained quiet, knowing there was nothing to say. She was glad to see the yard was full of cars and more relieved when she seen her mother's car. She had worried all the way here how she would handle this raw grief she had no experience with this kind of thing before, but found by being quiet let people cry and just be there must help.

Lupe took her face in his hands, "I never knew how much I depend on you, and you have always helped me out even in school, remember when other kids teased me and you would beat them up, I was afraid to fight because I was so much taller?" He looked at her again as if searching her face for the first time; it was like it finally dawned on him that here sat the most beautiful woman he was ever going to see. And she truly was beautiful. Nika said, "Lupe Lopez I have loved you since the first grade, but I am a proud Mexican woman and I do not chase after a man, he has to chase me and that's how it is." He had stopped crying and stood up stunned watching her as she walked in his house. He meekly followed.

Maria hugged her close to her and said, "What would I do without you? I depend on you more than I should at work I wonder if you know that." Nika tears running down her face, "You know I would do anything for you . . . . anything."

Maria stood tall and looked about her, "Let's all make a circle and hold hands, I want to pray for Senna. I have always believed God will take care of me, but this is asking a lot to have faith when your baby has been taken from you. I guess God needed Senna more than I do I don't understand. I have read and heard over and over, good comes from bad, where's the good in this?" Mr. Argo will you lead us in prayer.

Halfway through the prayer Maria started swaying, Mr. Argo helped her to a chair, she screamed, "Senna is not dead, Senna is not dead!" Lupe said, "Oh, Ma, stop it we have to accept this, tomorrow we will go to Police Chief Luis and have him try to help us find her. I know you think that your feelings tell you ah, stuff, but I am afraid this time you don't want to accept Senna being gone." "No. No, no, I felt her while we praying, she's in trouble, but she is not dead." Everyone in the room crossed themselves and then stood looking uncomfortable; they didn't know what to say. Lupe apologized to everyone, "Sometimes Ma gets these premonitions and I guess she is pretty accurate. Well I guess almost always, but I think Ma you're not accepting something as serious as Senna being dead." This started another round of weeping.

CHAPTER 13

DANA SLEPT THE WHOLE afternoon in the chair in Hank's room. He had his urinal and hoped he wouldn't have to move for a while. The therapy today plum wore him out, but he didn't want to wake Dana up she was sleeping so well. Rosa and the kids all came trooping in after school, chattering like magpies, all excited to see Dana. Dana woke up and looked at the time, "Mr. Why didn't you wake me up? You are past pain pill time you need those on time or it will be hard to get under control again." Hank growled, "You needed to sleep you have been going like a house a fire ever since you got here. Mikala go out to the kitchen and fix us all some lunch, then bring it in here, so I don't have to get up until supper."

Mikala brought cookies and milk, the kids sat on the floor, telling all about their day at school. Mikala said, "Guess what Miss Dana? We don't have school tomorrow, school conferences, so we can pick pecans all day, and then we can sell them on Saturday at the Farmers Market!" Hank said, "Hey Missy, you had better remember you are helping Miss Dana on Saturday. How are you going to do both things?" Mikala looking at Dana, "You said we would be done by 1:00, but I will stay all day if you want me." Dana laughed, "No, that's fine, we will get a bunch of pecans done tomorrow and maybe just maybe Mr. Hank will shell out a bunch for us."

Mikala turned to Rosa, "Ma after the Farmers Market could we—please—please—go to the dress shop and get the dress I want?" Rosa hitting her head, "My God I am so tired of hearing about this dress, your Dad is still mad over you not wearing grandma's dress, I guess we can get the DRESS, but you're going to have to figure out how to get around your Dad." Mikala started jumping up and down pumping her arm in the air, "First good luck we have no school tomorrow, then maybe I can have the new dress I want, this is turning out to be a good day." All three kids pumped the air with their hands and yelled, "Yippee."

Dana had to admit it was nice to have pizza for supper no clean up, she did make a chocolate cake and everyone felt full. It was fun just to sit on the front porch after supper and visit.

Hank wanted to go to bed early, the rest of the guys was watching a T.V. show. Dana got Hank cleaned up and in bed then she made herself eggnog with coconut rum in it, her night cap as she called it. She told everyone, "Good night, then headed for her screened in porch through patio doors that led from her room.

There was a door leading outside and just as she got settled with her drink and a cigarette, there was a scratching at the outside door, it was Bo dog. He had started doing that the second night she came out here. She wondered if he had stayed out here with Hank's wife, who had been gone for a few years, she might ask Hank sometime if they had Bo when his Liz was alive or maybe not. She was just starting to read the new mystery novel Rosa had gave her, when there came a knock at the outside door.

She said, "Buck well for heaven's sake come in, I'll go make you one of my night caps." He held up a beer bottle, "I don't think I could stand that creamy stuff you drink. What in the world? Bo what in the hell are you doing? You're supposed to be outside guarding the place." Bo opened one eye and pulled himself on his stomach a little closer to Dana. Buck said, "Does he stay here all night?" Dana by now was laughing, she put her bare feet on Bo's back and the dog looked dead again. She said, "No, he stays until I turn out the light and then he wants out, I did wonder if perhaps he was here when your mother was alive and maybe she sat out here at night?" Buck thought for a minute, "Yes, you're right she did come out here just like you do and I bet he stayed with her, well isn't that something."

They talked about Buck's mother for a while and then he said, "Ah, I'm kind of wondering if you will stay with us after Dad gets on his feet, you have worked wonders all ready. Well, what I'm trying to say is we all want you to stay. I mean I'll keep paying you even if Dad gets going again. He brought it up tonight—before—I go to bed—I usually visit a while, he's worried if he gets well you will take off. I guess he heard you get a phone call about another job, ah, is that, aha, true." Dana pleased, "Yes I did get a call, but I said it would be a month or so before Hank is up on his own so I would call them when you folks were done with me."

Buck uncomfortable, "Well we were kind of hoping you would stay with us for the winter, you sure don't want to go back to the cold weather and snow. Do you?" Dana didn't know how to answer. She was beginning to feel something for this man and that was a complete shock to her. She had went on a few dates after her husband died, but nothing very romantic. Most were men who she had known for years. She certainly didn't want to make an ass of herself over any man.

She said, "Buck I have to admit so far, I love it here, I never liked living in town nor do my girls, but it was too hard to stay on the farm, too much expense keeping up farm buildings, etc. I sold out and paid cash for the house in town and we were happy enough there. It's wonderful for me to go outside and putts around, and I like baking and cleaning. I am all excited about bringing some of your Mom's things down Saturday. I'm cleaning the bricks and I was afraid the smell might get to your Dad. You know what, thank you. I will see, but I think I would like to stay here too. You might be sorry you asked me, I have been told I can make other people nuts with my chattering and cleaning and not sitting down and being quiet sometimes, my first husband, I told you thinks I have a screw loose, he said I made him tired just watching me."

Buck relieved, "I think we can stand you just the way you are. I know I look forward to the darn good cooking. I guess we will come in for dinner tomorrow, we'll be working close to home and Sid wants to catch the Welch ponies for your company Sunday, their damn ornery little shits, but kids love them after Sid gets them straightened out." "Oh thank you this poor girl, that was awful in the airport, it was awful, and then you know what she thought I wouldn't want anything to do with her because of her trouble. Can you imagine, good grief? I guess they have to stay all together for fear of that man, they think he will try to steal the kids.

I all ready know your coming in for dinner you're Dad wants macaroni and cheese and hamburgers." Buck stood up and first ruffled Bo's hair and then patted Dana on the head, "You two don't stay up to late tonight, good night Dana and Bo you get your ass out and watch for unwanted visitors." Bo looked at him like who do you think you are? He didn't move.

When Buck left Dana thought you know old girl you should be leaving, this could be a heart break time for you, and then she thought Live for the Moment-enjoy every day as if it were your last. She let Bo out and went to bed.

CHAPTER 14

THE NEXT MORNING DAWNED bright and clear, Dana noticed most of the days were dry, not a lot of rain that was for sure. Actually she thought a little rain would be nice. She made breakfast for all the men and got Hank up and in his wheelchair. He decided to stay up and help with the pecans.

Rosa and the kids came with buckets. As soon as Dana was done with dishes she went out to help. Hank was already in his favorite chair shelling pecans. She couldn't believe how many pecans had fallen on the tarp. They got through one tree and decided it was time for a lunch break.

Dana had made a pan of bars while she cooked breakfast so they were wiping off sweat when a car drove up. It was Manuel's mother and Rosa's mother. The kids were thrilled. They said, "We wanted to meet this Dana nurse and see our old buddy Hank." Manuel's Mom said to Dana, "I lived here for many years now we live in town, no privacy, but my husband goes uptown everyday and sits around having coffee, and I have all the retired ladies come to my house for coffee. Then we watch T.V. and then we go to the Senior Center and play cards. We keep busy doing nothing; sometimes I miss this place, the peace and quiet." Dana enjoyed the steady stream of conversation and teasing that went on between the two women and Hank. The ladies were a copula of characters, they kissed Hank and their grandchildren, ready to go, when Manuel's Mom said, "Mikala do you have money enough for that new dress you want, just between, me and you I never liked my dress that much and you can tell your bull headed Dad I said get the new dress . . . . okay?"

After they left—the kids, Rosa, and Dana in her cowboy boots headed back to the second tree. Josh was the first to see something moving under the tarp, he jumped back grabbed his little brother and yelled, "Ma I see something under the tarp it's moving!"

Dana grabbed the rake and threw the edge of the tarp over. She nearly fainted when she seen a great big monster of a rattlesnake all coiled up. She yelled, "Where's Bo?" Hank yelled from the porch, "He's out with Sid, get a stick and kill it or take the hoe and cut its head off, nasty damn snakes I hate them too."

Dana went running to the gun closet in the kitchen, she came out loading a shotgun swearing a blue streak, Rosa, Hank and the kids were dumbfounded it looked like Dana had lost her mind. Her hair was standing straight up all around her sweat band and screaming hysterical, "You rotten son of a bitch, I'll see to it you never live another day, more swearing, then she screamed, Rosa you and the kids get on the porch I'm going to blow, this f . . . . up."

She shot the snake three times, still screaming, "She yelled none of you come down here until I get this f . . . . buried! She ran for the garage still cussing, came running back with a spade and started digging a hole." Hank was laughing and pounding his knee, tears running down his face. Rosa and the kids stood in shock; Rosa had her hands over Luke's ears.

All three kids kept looking at Dana and then at their mother, "Boy can Miss Dana ever say bad, bad, words, boy she really is mad, they looked at each other and then at wild Dana digging a hole, her hair all over her face, the kids whispered, "She looks like a witch!" Rosa trying not to laugh, "I guess we know our sweet, kind nurse, can get really crazy mad."

A pickup come flying in the yard, dust blowing around it. Buck jumped out, "What in the hell is going on we heard screaming and a gunshot clear out in the field. What's Dana digging?" Hank still laughing and by now Rosa and the kids were laughing too said, "Our nurse just blew a rattlesnake to smithereens, I'll tell you she can swear more words than even I know."

Buck saw the shotgun broke down and empty resting against the steps, it took him a few minutes to recognize Dana with her wild hair, and she had the rake and was raking pieces of a snake in the hole she dug. He approached her with caution, "Ah, are you alright?" "Alright, what do you mean alright? Do I look alright to you? No don't answer a snake and I mean a monster was hiding under a tarp all morning. We were all out here, happy, laughing having a good time. It just f . . . . made me mad, I don't know why this happened to spoil our day, now every day we will have to worry about a rattlesnake, I'm glad Bo wasn't home, it might have bit him."

Buck trying not laugh, "Well we will always make sure Bo is home after today, ah, can I put the gun away or is there something else you want to shoot today?"

He finally decided maybe he would dare put his arm around her, he did, she didn't even notice that he was sort of leading her up the steps to the porch, she kept looking back, it dawned on her then that everyone was looking at her real funny and Buck had his arm around her.

She yelled, "There's always two don't you know that, you see one rattlesnake and there's another one close by, by now she was stomping her feet!" Buck reassured her that he would go out and look under the tarps and around the garden while she went and sat down and maybe put her head between her legs

. Dana did sit down only she was shaking and lit a cigarette, blowing smoke in the air. She looked at all the shocked faces around her and burst out laughing.

Dana looked around her, the kids were sitting at her feet, looking up at her, with surprise on their faces, "You sure don't like snakes do you?" This from Joseph, while the other two snickered together.

Pete and Sid came driving up in a cloud of dust, all excited, "What's going on around here?" They could see Buck walking around the trees and garden with the leaf rake. Pete hurried to Dana's side sitting in a chair next to her, "What happened did you get bit?" The kids all chimed in, "No, she blew a snake up with a gun and then, giggling again, did a lot of swearing and looked like a witch. Sorry Miss Dana, but it was really funny." Pete patted her hand just as Buck came up the steps of the porch. Buck stopped in his tracks and looked at Pete; it was obvious he didn't like Pete by Dana.

Sid took in all the fuss and said, "Well, our nurse can shoot, well in case we have rustlers or something we will send her after them.

Everyone laughed again, looking at Dana to see if they were hurting her feelings, she laughed with them.

Little did they know the day would come when everyone of them would be overjoyed that Dana knew how to use a gun?

Rosa was in the kitchen getting dinner finished, Manuel came in the garage door, "What the hell happened here?" Rosa went into peals of laughter again, "It's Dana, you had to be here to see how funny it was, she was running around swearing, f . . . . ing this and f . . . . ing that, then she must have shot that snake about three times, and then she grabbed a shovel and buried it, all the time her hair was standing on end and with those cowboy boots and shorts on. Well, it was a sight to see."

The dinner of macaroni and cheese and hamburgers was a hit with everyone. Hank said, "That really hit the spot. I've been so hungry for mac and cheese. They cleaned up the leftover pies and cake for dessert. The men went back to work and Dana got Hank in bed for an afternoon nap. Dana, Rosa and the three youngsters went back to picking up pecans shelling them and filling sacks of both unshelled nuts and shelled out nuts.

CHAPTER 15

SENNA FINALLY, AFTER MAKING several wrong turns, made it to the back of the Wal-Mart parking lot. She was exhausted and her whole body was shaking from head to toe. She thought I have to calm down and think what to do? She tried to straighten her hair, looking in the rear view mirror, she thought I look terrible. She started paying attention to her surroundings; she noticed a truck stop across the road. Once again she asked God's help and decided the truck stop was her best bet, they would have public telephones, and maybe she would not be so noticeable. She thought they must have phone calling cards, too.

When she got out of the car she could hardly walk, stiff and sore, not only from driving, but spending part of the night before in a cold, wet place.

She crossed the busy street to the truck stop. When she got inside she went to a vending machine and got a can of pop and a candy bar, from another machine. She found the ladies rest room, her face in the mirror looked fine, and she was shocked, she still looked alright on the outside, except for the long sleeved sweater she had on. She pulled the sleeves way up her arm, it would look funny because it was now warm here—people might notice. She scrubbed her hands once more; they were still scratched, but not too bad. Her feet she could feel were in terrible shape, the shoes and Levis covered that part of her.

She walked up to the desk and asked to buy a calling card. The clerk showed her how to scratch off the card to find the numbers she needed. She knew Father John's phone number by heart because most of family and friends did not have phones, so they used the phone at the parsonage. The clerk told her where to find the pay phones; she carefully punched in all the numbers, under her breath she prayed —Please, God let Father John be home for lunch.

Myra answered the phone in the parsonage. Senna started crying when she heard Myra's voice. She said, "Myra, this is Senna Lopez." There was a dead silence on the phone, finally Myra choking said, "Who? Tell me again!" Once again Senna said, "Myra, this is Senna Lopez—I'm in a lot of trouble—I'm in Tucson Arizona and I desperately need Father John's help." By now she could hear Myra crying and yelling, "Father, come quick it's Senna Lopez, and she's not dead—even louder she's NOT dead."

Father John was just coming out of the bathroom from his shower before going to the Lopez's with the bad news, he kept saying,"What? What? Myra tell me again!" Myra was crying so hard she couldn't talk, she handed the phone to him. Senna puzzled said, "Father John, why is Myra crying?" He said, "Dear God, Senna, Senna, I don't believe it. Some man called your mother at work this morning and said you drowned in a lake, while you were on a picnic." Senna cut him off, "Father, I'm in a lot of trouble, that man must have been Damon. He thinks I drowned, but I got away." Crying harder now, "Father, he shot Carlotta, he took us to America to be prostitutes—we were locked in a big house. Please I don't know how long I can talk. I have no I.D. If the police catch me I will be arrested and put in a jail until I can be deported and that can take a long time I have heard. Father, I can't even cross the border to home without I.D.; sobbing now so Father John could barely understand her. I stole a man's car and money. I'm in Tucson Arizona at a truck stop. I still have the car, but I'm afraid the police will be looking for it by now. Please, please can you get me home from here, I was going to take a bus, but you have to have I.D. for even a bus ticket. If I ever get home I will pay this man back for his car and money—please help me."

Father John stood holding the phone in shock, finally, he said, "Let me think Senna I have an old friend living in Tucson—maybe—yes, yes, I think he will help. Where can I call you back? Is there a phone number there?" Senna found the number then carefully repeated it to Father. Father John wrote the number down and said, "Oh, thank God you are alive, Senna. I don't care what all you had to do to get home. We will get this all ironed out when you get here. If I don't call back in ten minutes—you call me back here—I will find a way to get you home . . . okay?"

When he hung up he ran around the dining room table about three times wringing his hands, "Myra you have to help me find Father Mark Kelley's phone number in Tucson. It's in my little book. I'm so shook up I probably can't even read!" She rushed to his desk and found his address book and gave it to him, she said, "Father I don't read all that good either." By now Father John took several deep breaths, trying to get his mind to accept everything he had just heard. He found Father Mark's name right away and was shocked when Father Mark answered himself—in his mind he thought, God you are HERE! I thought for a few minutes, you had deserted me, sorry. It was like God had sent Mark a message to pick up the phone. Father John explained as fast as he could about Senna and where she was in Tucson. He was relieved when Father Mark said, "Well, by golly, I have a young Priest visiting here right now, he can go with me. We will go right over and pick this poor girl up. Say, do you still have Myra?" "You bet! She is still hanging in there with me." From Mark, "Does she still make that Adobada thing with the pineapple? She used to wrap it in a tortilla. I can just taste it now." Father John, "Yes, yes, she still makes it." "Well, by golly, we will just bring your little girl right to your house if Myra can be persuaded to fix us an early supper." John overjoyed, "God Bless you, and of course, Myra will make Adobada for you, in fact, she's already pleased you asked about her. Senna is at a truck stop across from a Wal-Mart store, it must be the first Wal-Mart off the freeway, because she could see the sign that's how she got there. I will have her stand outside by the front door. Can you get her past the border?" Father Mark snorted, "They better not mess with me at the border, don't worry."

Father John was shaking when he hung up the phone. He had Myra dial the number for the truck stop, Senna answered on the first ring, when she heard someone was coming she started to cry again and then made herself stop crying, people were staring at her. Father John trying to act like this was just another conversation on a normal day said, "Don't cry, Senna. I need you to stay calm and normal looking until you get home than we will all cry with you. Wait outside by the front door Father Mark Kelley will come get you and he will drive you right to my house. He drives a BIG black car and I do mean big, that will be him. He can help decide what to do with the car you drove there . . . . okay?"

Senna hurried into the rest room and washed her face, then shoulders back she walked outside. Every black car that went by her heart would skip a beat. Boy, there are a lot of black cars she decided. It seemed forever when a really big black car drove up with two men in it. They both wore Priest collars, the younger one hopped out of the car and taking Senna's hand, "Are you Senna?" He then opened the back door of the car and helped her in. She collapsed crying turning to hiccupping sobs. The big car glided out of the parking lot.

She came to her senses and said, "Oh, Oh, I stole a car from a man. I have the keys in my pocket. I left the car in the back of the Wal-Mart parking lot. Will somebody try to hurt it if I hide the key somewhere on the car or under it?" Father Mark looked back at her, "Well, by golly we'll go get the car, Father Dan can follow us to my garage and we will keep it safe. Do you know this man?" The two Priests were stunned and horrified at the story she told them and then grim faced they told her, "You are a brave little girl and everyone will help you both at home and here in America. This is a wonderful country, however there are evil people, no matter where you go. Senna you have my word this Damon man will be brought to justice."

Senna asked Father Dan if she could use his cell phone while they were traveling to the parsonage garage. He handed it to her, she decided to call Father John and tell him she was safe. Myra answered, "Oh Senna, he is getting the car out so he can drive out to your mother's place. She went completely hysterical when she heard you were dead. She will be so happy. Oh, Father's here right now. Do you want to talk to him?" "Yes, please, Father, I was just going to ask you to tell my mother, could she bring me some clean clothes to your house. I am so dirty and I'm not positive that Carlotta is dead. I heard a shot and a scream and it sounded like her, so maybe we will have to wait until I meet with Police Chief Luis, something I want to do as soon as possible." Father Dan asked to speak to Father John, "Ah, Father, Senna's feet are cut and bleeding through her shoes. Do you have a doctor there who could see her when we get there she is afraid to see anyone here?" Father John assured both Senna and Father Dan everything would be arranged by the time they got here to John's parsonage. He told them as soon as they got across the border, he would get a hold of this man that Senna stole from to survive. He was going to call him personally, and he was sure the man could be persuaded to forgive Senna. Senna climbed in the back seat and was instantly asleep.

CHAPTER 16

FATHER JOHN HATED TO drive his beautiful car on gravel roads—it was his pride and joy—maybe a sin, but the car was all he owned in this world. He polished it every day and kept it inside all the years he had it. He usually walked up town or to his different church member's homes. It was a small town so he did not have far to walk in any direction. He had the car backed out and went back to the house to have Myra do some calling for him.

Myra was on the phone when he came in she waved to him putting her hand over the phone, 'I am calling several of our ladies to bring pot luck over to the church hall about 5:00 tonight. I told them we were entertaining two other Priests from Tucson.

"Did you tell them about Senna?"

"I told them not to tell anyone until you could get out to Maria's."

"Myra that's like putting it on the news around here, I need to hurry now—oh, well, that's alright, I guess. What I need you to do is call Tony Garcia to go with me out to Maria's. I am not good on those side roads and please call Dr. Juan to come if he can when Senna gets here, her feet are bleeding. Father Dan is very concerned about her."

Tony Garcia came through the door—Father John surprised, "How did you know I needed you? Let me guess Myra was busy on the phone—Myra, what would I do without you, it's like you read my mind?" Myra hanging up the phone snorted, "You need Tony to help you with Mr. Argo. He is going to be devastated. I think that's the word. He has no family here at all and what would I do without this job taking care of you? I would not be able to live without your money . . . . okay?"

Father said, "Tony you drive, I'm still shook up from all this excitement.

When they drove into Maria's yard there were cars everywhere, Father John had rehearsed all the way here how to tell Maria.

Lupe came out to the car, "Thank you Father for coming." Father John took of his hat and wiped sweat off his face, "Lupe help me, Senna is not dead. How can I tell your mother so she doesn't have a heart attack or something?" Lupe picked the little Priest up off the ground, "Tell me again, Senna's not dead?" Father said, "She got away from that awful man, but she thinks—ah—that he killed Carlotta. Lupe ran for the house yelling, "Ma! You're right! Senna's not dead—Father John tell her—Oh, my God I can't believe this. Ma just told us she had a premonition that Senna was alive. Father John stood in the middle of the room he held up his hand for silence because of course everyone was talking at the same time. He began, "Senna and Carlotta were held prisoners in a house of —ah—ill repute—this Damon man was angry with them both Senna and Carlotta for fighting him on what he wanted them to do—be prostitutes. He told them he was taking them out for dinner and then a drive through the mountains by Las Vegas, Senna happened to see a gun under the car seat, so she was prepared to get away. She tried to convince Carlotta with her eyes to come with her, but Carlotta probably could not believe this Damon would kill them."

Mr. Argo was holding his head and then slumped on the couch by Maria. They both were crying Maria with Joy and Artie with grief. Maria asked, "Where is Senna now?"

"Well, I have to tell you the whole story; she is on her way home from Tucson Arizona with two Priest friends of mine—ah—she stole a car from a cabin in Nevada. Now, wait don't everyone go to pieces—we will contact this man and the car has been put in my friends garage. We will work out how to get it returned and how to pay the man back. We don't think he knows his car is missing yet. You see if Senna went to the police in America they would maybe lock her up as an illegal alien and I guess it can take a long time before they get the paperwork done to deport them—that's why she is so afraid—she has no I.D. This Damon person lied about everything. He did not get them green cards."

"All the way out here I thought of Jesus raising Lazarus from his grave, wiping sweat off his brow with his handkerchief, I did not know how to tell this story, I can see our Father God, helping bring our Senna home and we hope we can stop this awful man, Damon, from ruining any other young girls life. He has even stopped in to see me before telling me how he could help these young women out of their poverty stricken lives. I actually believed him; he told me he had people who helped them learn good English and how to serve food and how to talk right and dress right."

"Let's all hold hands and pray." Lupe took Nika's hand and pulled her into the circle.

After the prayer, Tony Garcia asked Mr. Argo to come to his house for the evening he said, "You know how my kids love you. Please come." Lupe putting his arm around Artie on one side and still holding Nika on the other said, "I will do your chores Mr. Argo." Nika spoke up, "I will stay and help Lupe, and we will come to the church hall when we get done."

Father John asked Maria, "If she would ride back to town with him and Tony and hopefully Mr. Argo. Maria—"Myra will need help getting all the food over to the hall maybe you can help her and I almost forgot Senna asked if you would bring some clean clothes for her to town. The Priest's bringing her home has requested a doctor here to look at her feet. It seems that's how she got away by throwing her coat and shoes downstream and then running upstream in her bare feet, she spent part of the night hiding in tall grass." Everyone in the room was quiet for a few minutes and then everyone started asking questions at once. Father told them, "He didn't know much more about it yet. She had told him to set up a meeting with Police Chief Luis right away, but Myra had called Father in the car on Tony's cell phone and said Luis will be gone until Friday as his father-in-law had passed away, but he was sending one of his deputies to interview Senna today, so they could contact authorities in America about this Damon."

Maria, Mr. Argo, Tony and Father John got in the car and started out for town. They were all trying to comfort Artie, but realized only time heals grief. Maria thinking to herself—I wonder why I never noticed how attractive Artie Argo is. Well, my goodness I guess I have been so busy trying to make a living and keep a decent place for my children to live. Well, my goodness I never ever thought about any man, and here he is my closest neighbor. It seems like we are an old married couple, natural together. Well, my goodness, she reached out and took Artie's hand, looking straight ahead she thought this is right, yes, this feels so right.

When they got to Father John's garage, Tony said, "Artie, we can walk down the hill to my house. The misses are all cooking up a storm for an early supper, so we can visit a while without a lot of interruption . . . . okay?" "Artie looking embarrassed, Ah, Tony, ah, I would like to stay with Maria and help Myra, I think it would help me feel a little better and I want to be here when Senna gets here, ah, I guess she is going to shower and change clothes first, then Doctor Juan can do her feet, but I want to find out kind of what happened and if she thinks Carlotta is really dead." Through all this Maria never let go of Artie's hand. Artie had his arm around her shoulders. It was like they were glued together. Tony puzzled said, "Sure whatever makes this easier for you, Artie. You know you are always welcome at our house." Maria and Artie walked into the Parsonage together. Tony looked at Father and smiling, 'Well, I guess I didn't expect those two getting together, look at what a beautiful couple they make. He is so tall and proud, she's one fine looking woman, well, by golly I never noticed before, but their just right for each other!" Father John eyes twinkling, "You know God tells us always something good comes from something bad, sometimes I doubt God. Oh, I'm sorry Tony, I'm just human that's all, but today I see two miracles, first Nika and Lupe. If I was a betting man, I would say Lupe never noticed Nika as a woman, he's, ah, well he's a tomcat. That's all there is to it. Today he faced the real valley of death and I think he found out Nika was the only person he wanted at his side. Did you see the way they looked at each other? I like you Tony, was surprised at Maria and Artie, but I hope and pray they get together. They need each other, and their children are like brothers and sisters already. Wouldn't it be wonderful if four people get a new life out of this total disaster!" "Tony, "Yes, yes, yes oh my, now that you mention it. I can see what you're saying. Boy, I'm heading for home. I'll bet my girls will want to hear all about this. Well, it's not good if Carlotta is dead, but I never thought of it before. God does promise good from bad, I have learned a lesson today, better than any Bible Study, ah, well, gosh I'm sorry Father, but I mean if a person can see something good happening right before their eyes. Well, I will not forget this day."

Maria and Artie found Myra in the kitchen, sweat running down her face, "Oh Maria, she said, I am so happy for you. Senna is alive, praise the Lord!" Then she seen Mr. Argo standing with his arm around Maria, "Oh, Artie how could this happen, Oh, poor Carlotta, oh, I don't know what to say, damn, damn, why Carlotta? She is such a good girl. Don't tell Father I swore, but I'm so mad right now. Why do our young people want so much to go to America and earn big money?" Myra burst into tears. Both Maria and Artie told her they were just going to keep busy until Senna gets here and we don't know for sure if Carlotta is dead. Father had me call Chief Luis and he is gone, but will send his deputy so we can find out what's for sure is going on."

They all got busy helping Myra fold up tortillas filled with mouth-watering pork cut up, rubbed with her special sauce and then cut up avocado, pineapple and salsa added. Myra talking as fast as she worked, explained what all the other women were making, some Mexican wedding cakes and corn bread with chili. A feast to celebrate at least Senna was alive.

When Father John got in the house the phone was ringing. It was Senna calling from Kelley's car phone, "Please Father, oh I forgot, we made it just fine crossing the border. We are about an hour away and please would you call this Gary Valdez. I have his phone number right here and I want him to know right away what I have done before he finds his car missing and calls the police. I will too talk to him after I get cleaned up and talk to Chief Luis. She gave Father the phone number and address from the credit card and what she had copied down from the car registration. I will make everything up to him . . . . okay?" Father said, "I will be glad to do this Senna and don't worry we will all help you get this straightened out, your mother and Mr. Argo are here with me." Senna whispered, "Please, can I talk just a few minutes with my mother." When Maria came to the phone, Senna and Maria both started crying so hard, neither of them knew what they were saying.

CHAPTER 17

GARY VALDEZ WORKED FOR an investment firm in Las Vegas; he was
a consultant, with sales of stock and bonds for many investors. Gary
loved his job, but wished he had more time to spend with his two
darling babies, two year old Amy and four year old Trey. His mother
Mary cared for the children during the day until he got home then she
went back to her apartment close by to rest. It was not easy keeping
up with the two live wires.

There was a knock at Gary's office door and Andrea one of the
secretaries stuck her head through the door, "Gary, we are all going
to have a drink after work at Finn's Bar and Grill, to celebrate Blake's
new promotion. Will you be able to come? I know you like to get
right home, but we won't be long, I promise. Please you need to get
out more." Gary said, "You know what, I think I will join you, ever
since Lila died I just hate to leave the kids longer than I have to. My
mom is the best, but she won't admit it. The kids are busy little beavers
constantly asking questions and getting into mischief, nothing bad,
normal kids stuff, but my mom is not young and I know they wear her
out. I'll come for a little while . . . . okay?" Andrea closed the door and
then pumped her arm in the air with a secret smile on her face, "She
went, YES, maybe there's a chance for me with him yet, he is so darn
good looking, and those kids are adorable." After Andrea left, Gary
called his mom at home and asked if she would mind if he was two
hours late getting home. He explained about this little party at Finn's.
Mary was thrilled, "Of course I will stay. I will feed the babies and get
their jammies on. Then you can put them to bed. I am so happy you
are finally going someplace with your friends. The only way to cure
grief is to get back among the living. I know what I'm talking about.

After your Dad passed, I thought the end of the world had came for me, but now look every weekend. I go different places with my lady friends and cover your ears, sometimes I go out with men friends, so how do you like that?" Gary laughed, "What would I do without you, I love you. Thanks, I won't be too late. When Gary hung up the phone he was pleased not only that his mother was so great, but he kind of thought this Andrea was after him romantically. Embarrassed he thought, it's been over a year since I have even looked at another woman. I guess I did believe the end of the world came when Lila died of pancreatic cancer so fast. Life is too short, I'm only twenty eight years old, it's time to start living again.

Gary walked to Finn's Bar and Grill, when he came in everyone cheered, "It's about time you do something besides work!" Andrea sat very close to him making him feel a little uncomfortable, but it was kind of nice having a pretty woman, even though she was a white girl. He had seen too many disasters, when white and Latino got together. All the same it was nice to be out and talk to adults. There was much laughter and he noticed Andrea really downed the liquor. He stayed with one beer thinking he had to drive home. Andrea asked him all kinds of questions, "What do you do on the weekends, Gary? Do you stay home or do you go out to eat? What are the childrens ages again? I forgot, I know they're really cute from the pictures, that Trey with those big brown eyes. Well, he's a doll!" Gary opened his wallet to show the latest pictures and passed them around the table. He said, "Well, every other weekend we go up to my cabin by the lake. Sometimes my brother Barry and his wife Nina come up to the cabin. They have a boat so we go water skiing and kind of do nothing all weekend. The kids all love it. They have two teenagers, who really like playing with my kids. They treat them like they're dolls to play with, dressing Amy up and fixing her hair. Trey don't go for the dressing up part, they have to play cars with him. Anyway, we have fun. It's not much of a cabin, kind of simple, easy to take care of and we keep extra clothes and food there so we really only have to bring a few groceries. We have a washer and dryer in the cabin, Lila insisted on it, that way we don't have to drag wet clothes home."

Gary asked Andrea what she did on weekends. She told him about all the parties she went too, "I have a small apartment, my housework I do on Saturday mornings, then I go out for lunch with friends and then to the clubs at night," Gary asked if she went to church on Sundays, "She laughed I don't go to church. It's a bunch of hypocrite's, that's what I think. They are nice on Sundays, then all week do all kinds of mean stuff, like our boss. Oh, he's a big shot at his church, but look how he treats all of us, like we are slaves." Gary really uncomfortable now, "Ah, I kind of like him, sure he's tough, but I guess he has been fair to me." Andrea snorted, "It's because you go to his church. We all know that. He kind of favors you. Hastily, she added, I'm sorry, Gary, I should not have said that. He feels sorry for all the stuff that has happened to you. I guess we all admire how dedicated you were to Lila and the kids."

Gary stayed about an hour and then told everyone goodbye, "Invite me again sometime. This was fun. On the way home, he was a little envious of the good times they all seemed to be having at these dance clubs, but then he thought, I have the kids that's better than drinking every night.

CHAPTER 18

MARY VALDEZ WAS PUTTING together ingredients for a hot dish; she thought I'll make something the children will like and maybe a salad, she had baked a cake earlier in the day while the babies took a nap. They had went to the playground after lunch and thank goodness, they were tired enough to take a nap. Now they had made a house consisting of a blanket thrown over four chairs, they were both giggling, each with a flashlight, pretending they were reading a book they both knew by heart. Mary just had to laugh, her precious grandchildren, they kept her busy, but it also kept her young and active. The phone rang she thought, "Oh, bother I don't have time to chat right now . . . . hello." The man on the phone asked if Gary Valdez would be there or if this was the Valdez residence. —"Yes." He went on, "Ah I don't know how to explain this I am a Priest, Father John O'Malley from St. Sil Mexico, and then he went on to tell her about Senna and everything she had been through and that she wanted Gary to know she would pay him back and that there are several of us going to try to get your car back, he talked for several minutes with Mary asking a lot of questions, she explained she was Gary's mother and took care of his children because his wife had died, she asked for his phone number and then he remembered Father Marks cell phone, he told her to call that number, too."

Mary sat down totally confused she decided to call her other son Barry and have him come over, yes, maybe for supper. Barry answered, "Hi Ma, what are you up to?" She said, "I had the most fantastic phone call from some Priest in Mexico, he says some poor girl was leered to America by a bad man and he tried to make her and her friend be prostitutes. When they refused he took them supposedly

79

on a sightseeing trip up to Lake Irene, only he shot the one girl and the other one got away and found the key to Gary's cabin and stole Gary's old car and drove as far as Tucson with it. Now, two Priests from Tucson a Father Kelly and a Father Dan put Gary's old car in their garage and drove this poor girl home to St. Sill, Mexico. For the first time ever, Gary asked if he could go out for a drink with his co-workers and I told him of course that I would feed the kids and so forth. Now, I don't know what to do. I don't want to call Gary and ruin his evening, but maybe we should check this story out. It sounds so, I don't know suspicious, I guess." Barry said, "I think Nina and I will come over, we picked up sub sandwiches because the girls are at a game tonight with friends, we'll stop and get some more, that won't take long we should be there in a few minutes, I want to hear this entire story."

When Gary arrived home he was surprised Barry and Nina was there. After his mother told him about the phone call he said, "I think I will call Mr. Ring up at the lake and see if he can walk over and see if my car is gone. I can't believe all this; she found my credit card in the deep freeze and stole some of Lila's clothes, it doesn't make sense. How would she know where to look for the car keys and all the other stuff—wow?" Gary looked up the Rings' phone number and Mr. Ring answered, "Hello." Gary started explaining, "Mr. Ring could you walk over to my cabin and see if my car is there? Sure, I'll just wait; you should be able to see through the window in the garage." When Mr. Ring came back on the phone a little out of breathe he said, "My God, Gary, your car—is gone—what the Hell!—You don't have it?" Gary answered, "This is about the weirdest thing that's ever happened to me, he then went on to tell Mr. Ring about the phone call from Mexico." He heard Mr. Ring in the background trying to tell Clara what it was all about, he heard Clara demanding to talk to Gary. Mr. Ring said, "Ah, I think Clara's lost her mind, but she has something to tell you, and now she has me wondering about something too, here's Clara." Clara said, "Gary, I told my old fool here that a boy now grown up who used to live here with his folks, well he's some big shot in Las Vegas I guess, but I don't care a tiger never changes it's stripes, he was a monster as a child, and I'll bet he has not changed, anyway he was up at the Park this morning, him and two other guys, one was black, they were looking all over in the grass, I took the dog out and pretended like I didn't see them, but they went down to that bridge by the creek and was trying to drag something out of the water, you mark my words, anything that Damon Hutt is involved in will be of the devil." Mr. Ring grabbed the phone from Clara, "Sorry Gary, Clara might be right about all this I made fun of her the last two times she claimed to see Damon hanging around here, but maybe I'd better check this out."

Gary told his family about this strange conversation with Clara Ring then he said, "The thing is—I do a lot of consulting on hedge funds for Damon Hutt—well, he has some accountant in Texas that sends me checks and he always is so pleasant and kind of—well—let's me make his investment decisions. I'm getting kind of worried here, ah Mom does Aunt Bella still live in Mexico I guess I have never asked you much about her I can only remember going to see her once." Mary said, "She's so crippled up she doesn't go anywhere anymore. She well—is kind of ashamed of her living conditions, I was there two years ago and thought she had a nice little place there—no running water—, but it was peaceful and quiet, I liked it." Gary thought a minute, "Barry do you think we could all take your van and go down to Tucson or maybe go on down to see Aunt Bella first, then pick the old car up and you could drive the van home? Do you think we could—well—maybe go this weekend? I don't know why I'm saying this, but I, ah, want to meet this girl, Senna, don't ask me why because I don't know it's just a feeling I have." They all looked at him with surprise and then Mary crossed herself, "Gary this will sound dumb, but if God led this girl to your cabin, your credit card and your car, ah, I think I know what you're feeling, I think it is essential that we meet this girl and her family. I don't think it's a long ways from Bella's to St. Sill, but I will look it up." Barry said, "Why not? Let's all go there's room in the van and coming home we will have lots of room."

That night Gary laid awake wondering about this day, he was worried that Damon Hutt was one of his best clients. What if he was a crook? Gary never liked to think bad of a person, but if he admitted the truth, he really didn't like Damon, he only seen him once or twice a year and that was enough. Gary had always thought somewhere deep inside that Damon was a phony, he acted so nice, but Gray thought I wonder what's under that pretend person shell.

CHAPTER 19

SATURDAY MORNING CAME BRIGHT and early to a sleepy Dana. She hopped out of bed excited to get the men off to a funeral so they could start on the living room project. She got Hank up and the night before they had went through his closet to find his dress suit, a beautiful western cut, black suit, so they decided to dress him up in his finest and then eat breakfast with his jacket off. She scrambled some eggs and made toast, Buck was already in the kitchen making coffee. He said, "You know what I think Dad and I will leave a little early and drive up to the pasture—ah—Dana what do we do about bathroom breaks?" She told him, "We have it all worked out. I made a bag and hung it on the side of his wheelchair, it's deep enough. We hid a urinal in the bottom and then put a big box of Kleenex on top, well I hope you won't need anything else, this will be quite a day for him, I know he's looking forward to being with you for the day." Buck amused, "And I think a certain Miss Dana wants us out of the way as soon as we can go, so you can start playing house, am I right?" Dana admitted he was right.

As soon as Buck and Hank was in the car Dana hurried to get the shampoo machine out. She filled it with the chemicals while Mikala and Rosa pulled out the furniture. Dana took an old paintbrush and started putting the acid on the fireplace bricks, after she had it covered; she decided to let it set a while, she took the curtains down and fluffed them up in the dryer after she shook them out. Rosa had a lot of the white rug done already and Mikala was polishing all the end tables and coffee table. Dana went back to her brick job and found the smell not as bad as she thought, and to her surprise the soot and dirt wiped off so easy. The fireplace was beautiful, all white bricks; she was so pleased the whole room was looking better. She decided to get the ladder from the garage and do the outside of the windows while Mikala did the inside; Rosa seemed to like running the shampooer. Working together made the job seem a lot easier or maybe it was Mikala's enthusiasm that kept them laughing all morning. After everything was shiny clean Dana went upstairs and started carrying down all the silk flowers beautiful vases and end tables that had been stored away. Rosa and Mikala insisted they carry stuff down and Dana could put it where she wanted it. By 1:30 with the three of them sweating the room looked beautiful.

Hank and Buck drove up and everyone helped Hank to his wheelchair; he was exhausted, until he put his hand up, 'Stop" He said "Oh, my God I never thought I would see this house look like this again!" Buck stood with his mouth open in shock, "It's like Ma came back to life." Rosa, Dana and Mikala stunned fell to their knees by Hank. Dana whispered, "I'm sorry maybe I have overstepped my bounds." "No, he said holding her hand, this is the best thing you could do for me." Buck shook his head in agreement, "Well it's darn nice to come home to this beautiful room thank you girls." Hank turned to Buck, "Give these three girls money to buy what they want in town and you girls go have fun on me and Mikala you get your fancy dress. Bring home hamburgers and fries from that hamburger place. Buck will put me in bed." All three women changed clothes and were gone.

The kids went to the farmers market to sell their pecans. Rosa and Dana went to the lounge and ordered margaritas Rosa said, "I can have one that won't hurt me." Dana had two and they laughed over the morning like to silly school girls. They went to the farmers market and the kids had sold all their pecans so they all crowded into the store with the fancy dress while Mikala tried hers on Dana found a pant outfit with straps over the shoulders and a ruffle around the top bright flowered pink and white slacks for the bottom then she looked at the price. Now way she thought.

That night Buck had a date to take Billie to the dance in town. Sid and Pete came out all cleaned up too. Pete came in the living room where Dana had settled Hank, she had rented two funny movies, and Martha was coming over too, Pete said, "Well why don't I stay with you tonight maybe you will need help getting hank to bed." Buck whirled on Pete, "No I thought you were going with Connie." Pete shrugged he looked at Buck like what's with you, "Connie can live without me for one night." Buck said, "You come with me, I need you to bring the pickup to town. I might have to come home early that mare is acting funny in the barn; maybe going to have trouble. Billie and Connie are picking me up. I am not in the mood to go out, but she had a fit so I guess I'm going." Once again, Pete amused winked at Dana smirking looking at Buck, "Okay, Boss whatever.' Out the door they went.

Dana made popcorn. Rosa, Manuel and the kids came over to watch the movies they all had a good laugh. Hank got tired after the second movie so everyone went home. Dana was really tired too so after she got Hank settled she pulled on a pair of old soft pajama's and fell into bed. She was sound asleep when someone tapped her on the shoulder, sitting up disoriented; she looked up to see Buck standing by her bed. He said, "I'm sorry to wake you up-ah-my young mare is trying to have her foal and Manuel and I have too big of hands to help her. I was wondering if you can help us." Dana jumped out of bed pulling on her shoes, her hair was standing on end all over her head. She grabbed a headband then said, "There's KY jelly in your dad's medicine cabinet grab that for me will you? What time is it anyway?" Buck astonished, "It's about midnight and KY jelly—what's that?" Dana said, "Oh I'll put that around the baby and hope he or she pops out." Buck did as she said. When they got to the barn, Dana went to the struggling mare dropping to her knees making soothing sounds to the horses. She ran her hands around the foal and after a few pushes from the mare, the foal did pop out. Dana was patting the horse saying what a good girl she was. Buck and Manny said, 'Dana, she might get mean better come out of there. Buck has coffee ready." Like a shot the horse jumped up her ears back and started for a moving Dana who jumped up and over the corral fence right into Buck's arms. Dana not even paying attention to Buck said to the mad horse, shaking her finger, "You dumb ass —what the hell—get back there and lick your baby right now, you have responsibilities! Now get with it.!" Buck was still holding Dana. He sat her down and said "Let's have some coffee in the office, it looks like you need some." Then he started to laugh, Dana was covered in blood and straw, her hair standing on end, turned around to see Billie, Connie and Pete standing there staring at her. She stood a minute than threw her arms in the air dancing around. She started singing, 'Wild Thing'. Everyone but Billie howled with laughter. As dignified as she could Dana left for the house thinking—what next? She grabbed a clean nightgown and robe and went to the shower. She even had straw in her hair. When she came out of the bathroom Pete stood leaning against the steps. He said, "You in love with him?" Dana stopped in her tracks, "Who?" Pete looking at her, "I mean, Buck." Dana stood a minute thinking, "Well I guess he's pretty easy to love." Pete said, "I was kind of hoping it was gonna be you and me. We are the hired help." Dana clearly surprised, 'Well, Pete I think you had better keep your Connie she's a looker and nice too." Another voice from behind them, "Dana you sleep in—in the morning, I'll make breakfast." Dana whirled around it was Buck and the look he gave Pete—blue eyes as hard as nails. Dana pretending to walk normal to her bedroom closed the door leaning against it. She thought, Oh, dear God, I didn't see that one coming. I've been working and living with all women I forgot what it's like to be around macho men. In bed she hugged herself. It felt real good to be in Buck's arms—too good, but she thought I'm not going to mess around in that Billie's territory. Ha.

CHAPTER 20

THE NEXT DAY DANA did sleep in and then she got her dress up clothes getting ready to meet Santiago's for dinner at the lounge in town. She fussed over her makeup, finally going out to the dining room. She was a little nervous about the night before with Buck and Pete, but decided to pretend nothing happened. Everyone was at the table. Sid looked like he had just came home. Buck had made oatmeal and toast. Hank was at the table all dressed in his good clothes. They all whistled when she came in she went, "Ha, you thought I couldn't dress up once in a while. Buck how's our baby this morning? Was it a boy or girl?" Buck laughed, "He's fine and his mother wants to see you to thank you." "I'll bet she wants to see me so she can try to take another bite out of my butt!" The rest of breakfast was normal. Dana admitted she was a little nervous about meeting Don Santiago considering she had stuck her nose in his family business. Mikala came in the back door and asked Dana if she was ready. All the men asked, "Ready for what?" Dana said, 'I'm going to church with Mikala." Looking at Buck, "I decided I would take you up on a morning off. I see you even made Hank's bed." Buck surprised, "Are You Catholic?" "No, I go to the Lutheran Church at home, but I thought maybe a few words with God might be appropriate today. It certainly can't hurt me."

After church, which Dana had enjoyed they went to the lounge. Hank, Buck and Sid were already there. When the Santiagos came in Lucia and the children all were trying to hug Dana at once all except Josh, he kind of stood back. Don Santiago shook her hand and his wife threw her arms around Dana then Josh came and hugged her. After introducing everyone, they all relaxed and had a good time. Sid had shown up for dinner. He took one look at Lucia trying to look cool, but Dana could tell he could not take his eyes off Lucia. Hank insisted on paying for everyone, "Now, I want all of you to come out to the ranch. Sid has a surprise for you."

At the ranch Sid took Lucia and her children plus Rosa's children out the barn to ride the horses he had rounded up.

Dana and Lucia's mother sat on the porch, smoking while Don, Hank and Buck talked in the kitchen. Lucia's mother thanked Dana again, "We should have known Richard was a bully. Now we are so afraid he will show up and try to steal the children. It's a nightmare. I keep thinking how could we not know what Lucia was going through? We are almost down to living like prisoners in our own home. Don has a restraining order on him, but that's not worth the paper it's written on."

Dana had made a cake on Friday that has to stay in the refrigerator for a day, a filling between layers and a luscious frosting. She served sandwiches and cake when all the kids came in. Their little cheeks were red and they were having such a good time together.

When it was time to leave all the children hugged Dana and Lucia's mother put her arms around Dana and whispered, "You are a Godsend for us." Lucia, a little shy held out her hand to Sid, instead Sid gave her a big bear hug, "You come back and bring the kids. This was the best of days." All the children ganged up on Sid and took him down laughing then hugging him. Sid looked embarrassed, but pleased and obviously did not want them to leave.

That night everyone was getting ready for the barbeque at Billie's house when Sid came out all dressed up. Dana went "Wow, who's at this barbeque that gets you all excited and fixed up?" He mumbled, "I'm not going to the barbeque—ah—well-ah-I'm kinda going someplace else." Buck and Hank snickered, "Like El Paso, maybe?" Dana stopped in her tracks, wheels turning in her head, "Well well, you will never find a nicer prettier girl than Lucia. Praise the Lord! She does need something to look forward too."

CHAPTER 21

THE BIG BLACK CAR glided to a stop by Father John's parsonage. Lupe behind Marie running her hands in the air sobbing, Senna, Senna—pulling Senna in her arms, "Oh, let me look at you. It's a miracle! You are such a brave girl-it's a miracle! I thought you were dead." One look at Senna's bleeding feet, Lupe gathered her in his arms, "Senna, Dr. Juan is coming after you have had a bath. Oh, dear God over and over he said it as he sat Senna on the bathroom stool." Maria started the water. Maria took off Senna's shoes, she was horrified. Senna could not stop sobbing while her mother undressed her like a baby and helped her in the tub. Tears running down Maria's face, they looked at each other like they had never seen each other before. Maria handed a Kleenex to Senna. Senna leaning back whispered, "I am so ashamed. How can I face people? I was a prostitute and now a thief. How can I face the church and town people." Maria said, "Sssh, everyone thinks you are so brave, so full of courage to get away was God's plan for you to help others. God will tell you what to say and you will see he has some kind of plan for your life, please just relax and soak your tired body."

Myra knocked on the door. "Dr. Juan is here also the deputy from Chief Luis. Can you come out?' Maria helped Senna to a chair outside the bathroom where Dr. Juan started medicating and wrapping her feet. The deputy, hat in hand, "Ah—Chief Luis asked me to keep this man's name quiet if you can. He has telephoned a friend in America, some big shot important FBI man to start looking into what you told Father John and Father Mark. Chief Luis will interview you on Saturday when he gets home. They are going to—ah—I don't understand it all; I think they're going to try to catch this man in the act."

Lupe came in pushing a wheelchair down the hall, "Everyone is waiting to see you over to the Parish Hall. Father John, Mark and Dan are waiting for you to come to bless the food. The church ladies have made a feast." Senna crying again, "Oh Lupe, how can I face them my shame it is deep?" The doctor, deputy and Lupe all protested at once, "No, no, you must not feel this way, they say you are a very brave girl." Just then the phone rang, Myra answered," Hello this is Gary Valdez. My mother gave me this number to call about a young girl in care of a Father John and—ah—I believe a Father Mark." Myra all excited, "Yes, yes she is here. Please Mr. don't charge or how you say it prosecute our Senna. We will all help to pay you back, please!" Gary shocked, "Please believe me. I am so proud to help this poor girl to safety she owes me nothing. ah—please, can I speak to her?" Myra handed the phone to Senna, she kept shaking her head no, and finally, "Hello, this is Senna Lopez, then the tears came again—hiccupping. I am so sorry for stealing from you. You see that was the only way I knew to get away. I was terrified to go to the police because I was an illegal alien." Gary said, "Whoa girl. I am happy beyond belief to have helped you a fellow countrymen, you owe me nothing. When I think of how terrified you must have been, well, it makes me mad that someone in America would do this to you and your friend. I am sad to tell you these terrible things have happened to a huge number of Mexican people especially young girls, sick—excuse my language S.O.B's." "Thank you, Mr. Valdez, the deputy police would like to talk to you now, once again, thank you, God bless you." She handed the phone to the deputy who explained where his car was located. Then told him about the Chief asking everyone to keep this terrible man's name quiet as the American FBI was in on it now and they don't want, "How you say it . . . to spook him?" Gary agreed this was good advice. Then he said, "My family and I are going to come to Mexico on Saturday to visit our Aunt and then they planned on a trip to St. Isles Sunday to meet Senna.

Senna's face turned red holding her mother's hand she whispered, "I can't, I can't meet his family I feel so unclean."

Lupe started pushing Senna out the door and down the hill to the Parish Hall before she changed her mind. She kept looking up at him and her mother with desperate eyes. When they entered the hall everyone clapped and cheered, many grabbed her hand and some leaned down and kissed her. Finally she said tears running down her face, "I am so ashamed of leaving here looking for a better life. I found out I had a wonderful life right here. I will be grateful for the rest of my life to all of you for helping me believe in the God who carried me out of Hell, who stayed with me no matter what selfish thing I had done. God bless all of you and believe me there is a loving God. I ought to know he helped me get here. For some unknown reason—yet, God saved my life and I hope I can live up to his expectations. A lot of tears were shed in that hall, but a lot of hope for struggling poor people who needed a boost in their belief in a caring, loving God. The deputy stood up and asked everyone to keep quiet about the man who was being looked into in America. Then he added, "Please, I just hate to tell you this, but we must keep Senna coming home a secret. Her life may be in danger. Chief Luis and I want to hear from any of you if you see this man around here again."

Mr. Argo came to sit by Senna, she once again crying, "Mr. Argo, I am not sure what happened to Carlotta. She might have lived through all this. I don't know for sure anything, she did make friends with an older gentleman who wanted to save her and maybe she got away. I don't know. I wish it were so." Mr. Argo put his hand over his heart, "Senna, I wish Carlotta could come home like you, but somehow I feel she is dead. This feeling came over me as your mother insisted you were alive. We old people sometimes do know things. I feel terrible to think I wish it was my Carlotta sitting here holding my hand, but I must be grateful at least you are alive and home. I will help you anyway I can and I have to tell you I feel this strong attachment to your mother. I'm embarrassed to say, but I need her." Senna shocked, "I can't believe you and Mama, oh, I hope that is true. When I was a little girl, I used to pretend you were my daddy, and you see, I don't remember my father. You always had such a nice farm and Carlotta had lots of nice clothes. I was also envious of your nice car." Maria sat down just then, "Senna, what are you saying?, "You wanted a father, you never said, oh my, I was always working. I know . . . I know I blamed myself for you wanting to leave." Taking Mr. Argo's hand, Maria said, "I'm pretty thick-headed sometimes. I did not notice Mr. Argo until today when I needed support and I finally noticed what a handsome man he is." My goodness, blushing she looked at Artie. Senna's eyes started to sparkle and she laughed standing up with her big feet in Father John's bedroom slippers, she hugged Mr. Argo and Maria together,

"You two make a cute couple." Mr. Tate and his wife came over, Maria introduced them to Senna telling her this was the new people who bought the hotel. Mr. Tate shook Senna's hand he said, "Miss Senna we are looking for a waitress for the hotel dining room I wonder if you would be interested. You speak very good English and we need a girl with your good looks and nice personality. If that does not work out for you or us we will find you something else to do in the hotel. We all love your mother. She has helped get the hotel in shape and knows a lot of the business of managing a hotel and she knows the customers from being there so many years." Senna close to tears again, "I would love to work for you. I can come tomorrow." "No" they said, "Rest a few days. How about Friday to start and did I hear correct the man that helped you will be coming on Sunday? Maybe you could bring him to our hotel's dining room for dinner?" "Yes," He is coming to visit his aunt in a town close to St. Isle so his whole family will come with him. I will pay you back if I can treat them to a dinner. Please, it would mean a lot to me." "Of course, we can work out something."

The deputy came to Senna with his cell phone, "Senna, the man whose car you borrowed gave me some new clues about this man. We won't mention his name, he would like to talk to you for a few minutes." Senna reluctant took the phone, "Hello, Mr. Valdez, I want to thank you again and I would also like to invite you, your wife and children and whoever else you want to bring to a Sunday dinner at the hotel in town, please can you come?" Gary Valdez, "Ah, Senna, my wife died last year. She had a fast moving cancer that's why you found her clothes in the cabin." Horrified Senna said, "I am so sorry. I did look at all your pictures in the cabin and you were—well—such a beautiful family. Who takes care of your children?" Gary sighing, "My mother has been wonderful. She comes every day since Lila passed away. I wanted you to know what I told the deputy. I called the old couple that lives to the east of my cabin to see if my car was really gone and this lady, a Mrs. Ring had a lot of things to tell me about Damon Hutt and it wasn't good. Okay now, I have to confide something else to you without breaking client confidentiality. I will hint around how I know this man and then see if you can explain what I'm going to tell you to your Police deputy there. I work for an investment firm in Las Vegas. I handle a lot of really wealthy people's money. I watch their investments and make decisions' as to what would be their best money making stock or mutual fund. I can't tell you anymore, however, I think with Mrs. Ring's evidence and my firm, the police might get on the right track a little faster. The other thing I want to ask you if you have a phone number that I can call if I hear more about your case." Senna said, "No, I don't have a phone. When I get situated with money I will buy a phone." Gary asked, "I was wondering is there any money left from your travels?" "Oh yes, yes I still have on hundred dollars to send you. Please would you keep that money and go buy a prepaid cell phone, then call me at this number when you get it so I can have your number. Is there some place in your town where you can buy a phone?" "Well, yes there is, but it's terrible expensive. I can't spend your money like that." "I insist you do this, I want to keep track of you. I admit I am worried for your safety and so is your Police Chief. Can you still get one tonight and call me back?" Senna asked Tony Garcia if it was possible and he left for the local gas station right then. Within a half hour Senna had a phone. She called Gary Valdez right away with the number.

Lupe said," I think it's time for us to go home so Senna can rest." Maria and Senna did a lot of hugging before they left and Mr. Argo went with them. Maria insisted he come home with them and sleep in Lupe's room. Lupe would sleep on the couch. Before Lupe left he went to Nika and asked her to come outside with him to wait for his mother and Senna. He did not know how to say to Nika the words he wanted to say, it came out in a rush of words," Nika—ah—ah—I never knew how I felt about you until—well—until you drove up to the farm today. I could not believe it when you said you loved me. I thought you were too good for me. Everyone says what an angel you are and how beautiful you are, so I didn't think I had a chance, well damn it! I want to say, I love you too. Now there I said it, if you didn't mean what you said that's alright, but I sure hope you love me." Nika threw herself in his arms. They were both shaking after a kiss that went on until Maria and Senna showed up. Embarrassed they broke away. Maria clapped her hands and went, "Praise the Lord! I am so happy. I never thought I would see this day. The two of you belong together."

Everyone was exhausted when they got to Maria's. Mr. Argo did stay. The next morning Maria made breakfast for all of them. Mr. Argo decided he must go home and see to his animals and Lupe followed him home to help. Maria was staying with Senna, who went right back to bed after breakfast.

When Mr. Argo got home the yard was full of cars. Neighbors were there doing chores and all kinds of women bustling around the kitchen. He had built a new house for his wife before she died it had a large living, dining area combined and two nice bedrooms with a bath in between. He apologized to the women, "I am not much of a housekeeper. This house feels so empty I stay outside a lot and never clean like I should." The women were already vacuuming and doing dishes that were piled up on the counter. Mr. Argo went right to the telephone to call his sister-in-law who lives many miles away. She was his wife's sister and kind of a bossy lady, "Anna, he said, "I have bad news, then he went on to tell her about Senna and Carlotta." She started crying, "Oh, Artie, how can this be? Why my own Dahlia left yesterday with this nice man who offered her a chance to go to America and work in his hotel. He will get her a green card just like he did our two neighbor girls. They flew here with him and stayed at their ma's place overnight. They each brought a thousand dollars home to their folks, they were so happy. So Dahlia and Rae left with him yesterday, in his fancy SUV. No, this cannot be true what they tell you, he is such a nice man." Artie dreading the answer, "What is this man's name?" Anna, "His name is Damon Hutt, very handsome and very rich. Why?" Artie all confused now, "Anna someone is at the door I must go." Anna said, "I forgot to tell you Dahlia has one of those fancy cell phones. She has already called and said they are staying in a beautiful house where they will learn more English and how to serve food." Mr. Argo was shaking so badly when he hung up wondering . . . could Senna be lying? No, no her story would be hard to make up. He thought only a minute and then dialed the deputy's number. Mr. Argo told the deputy everything he had heard on the phone. The deputy quiet for a minute said, "I think I had better call Chief Luis. This is getting too complicated for me and I do believe Senna, she would not lie. I know she is an honest girl." Mr. Argo took Lupe outside and told him what his sister-in-law had told him. Lupe running his hands through his hair, "How two happy girls can come home and Senna says she was a prisoner, I don't understand. Are you saying you don't believe Senna?" Mr. Argo shook his head, "I don't know what to believe anymore. I called the deputy and he is going to call Chief Luis to come home. He says this is way over his head."

CHAPTER 22

LUPE DROVE HOME WORRIED he woke Senna up to tell her what was going on now. Senna and Maria both started crying, Senna said, "So now they think I am a liar, how can I prove this? I have no one to back me up except you and Mama, oh why, did I have to mess my life up this way?" Senna's cell phone rang. She had to look for it and found it in her bag of clothes. It was the deputy, "Senna, Chief Luis is going to come home earlier can you meet with him today about 4:00." Senna still weeping, "Please I did not lie even though everyone will think I have made this whole story up." The deputy said, "Chief Luis believes you and so do I. We are going to get to the bottom of this."

Lupe drove Senna to the police station at 4:00. The Chief asked Lupe to have a chair outside while he talked to Senna. He brought a can of soda in to Senna and asked her to relax and take as long as she needed to tell her story and he asked her permission to tape the conversation. Senna looking down at the table, "Yes sir, I don't want my family or Father John to hear this please.' He reassured her it was for the investigation, but if they caught this man would she testify against him in a court of law?" Holding her head between her hands—her voice—almost a whisper—yes—I Pray to God everyday that I would never see him again—ever." She looked up then eyes flashing "Yes, I'll do whatever it takes to catch him." Chief Luis smiled, "Good girl, now let's hear this story." Senna started in, "There was an ad in our hometown paper about jobs as models or movie stars. I went to meet this Damon at the hotel dining room. Carlotta, who was prettier than me wanted to come with me, we were really excited. He seemed to be such a nice man explaining he would get us green cards and we could make a lot of money especially if we got in the movie business. He said there were all kinds of work for kitchen and dining room help and cleaning jobs paid twenty dollars an hour. He told us that he had sponsored several girls and they came home with lots of money or married a rich American. He also said our visa's would be good for six months. We both signed a paper and met him at the hotel the next morning. He drove us in a white van to an airplace. I don't know where we were—we were so excited to be in an airplane. He was the driver or what do you call it—the pilot. It did not seem to be a long ride, but it was fun. We landed out in the country somewhere—dry looking land. We were met by another van and ended up at a beautiful house. A Mexican woman met us at the door, very nice, spoke to us in Spanish, then a beautiful woman came and introduced herself and said we would live with her for a while. She would teach us better English and show us how to fix our hair and wear makeup. She had beautiful clothes for us to try on. We both helped in the kitchen while she explained the various dishes we used and how to serve food. Every day we took vitamin pills so our skin and bodies would look nice. There were several Mexican people working there, they all told us how happy they were to find good jobs and to be able to send money home to their families. After two or three days Carlotta and I felt so happy, so relaxed, happy I don't know I can't describe the feeling. Of course, I found out much later the vitamins were drugs." Chief Luis stopped her there, "You believe you were drugged. Why, I didn't think of that, no wonder you thought everything was so beautiful. Do you know what kind of drug? Please continue on this whole story is starting to make sense to me now." Senna feeling braver now, f "Damon came to get us and we flew again in his airplane to Las Vegas, at least that was on the sign where we landed. A man picked us all up, George, a big negro man, he drove us to a mansion or castle with fence all around, gates electric, I think, I have never seen such a fancy place. There were water fountains outside and a huge pool. The house had three levels, we were to live upstairs. As we walked through we could see a fancy room with all kinds of couches and chairs and little tables. They showed us to our room, beautiful rooms upstairs for the girls, then several other girls came in and sat on the bed all chattering about how lucky we were to be with them. They said, "They made about a thousand dollars for a week." Carlotta got really excited she couldn't believe all this. I was a little leery about all this; it was too much to take in for my mind. A lady named Mary Belle came to meet us and said, "It's time to eat it. Sounds like you girls have met everyone. Feel free to come to me with any questions, my room is on the second floor. Enjoy your dinner, I will visit you later about your duties." After dinner or supper to us the other girls hurried upstairs and changed clothes—skimpy clothes is how I would describe their outfits. They went down the stairs laughing and giggling to the first floor. I felt like I was floating on air. Carlotta said she felt the same way, we could not believe it.

The next day Mary Belle came and got us we were brought to a huge closet with every size clothes gorgeous dresses some long lots of really short skirts with cut out tops showing a lot of—ah—cleavage. I knew right then we were in trouble. My mind felt so fuzzy when she explained we would be entertaining gentlemen callers the first night and to watch what the other girls did. The first night I was dressed in a long strapless ball gown. I just sat with different men and drank pretend champagne with them. The next morning everyone slept very late than did their nails, some sat by the pool. Carlotta whispered to me that she had made a hundred dollars the night before. I was horrified she was so excited. I said, "Carlotta, I don't think I can do this. I have to go home." She laughed at me and said try it you won't believe all the money we can make, it's a hundred dollars per man.

That night I was sent to a beautiful room, candles all over, soft music playing, when one of the men I had sat with the night before came in, he said, "Girl, you are so beautiful. I thought you might help me I need some new excitement." I did not know what to do. I did see a bottle of oil on the dresser so I asked him to take off his clothes and I started rubbing his back. He wanted me to rub more than that, but I confessed I had never done this before and I didn't know what to do. He dressed and went out. He went to Mary Belle I could hear him and asked for a more experienced girl. I was shaking all over. I started to leave the room when another man came in and asked me to take my clothes off. All he wanted to do was look at me naked. I shook all the time I spent getting out of that long dress and the skimpy underwear they had me wear. All he did was run his hands over my body then he kissed me all over, I thought I was going to throw up. He hugged me and gave me a hundred dollar bill, he said, "Hide this, it's for you and only you don't tell Mary Belle."

The next day I started throwing up by evening, I was desperately sick. I was allowed to stay in my room, I could keep no food down, that's when after two days I realized I was being drugged because my mind cleared up and I knew I had to leave this place. I demanded to see Mary Belle and Damon. They listened as I become hysterical screaming, "This is not what you said, this is a whorehouse and I will not stay here, I want out right now!" They each held my hands and explained they would find me another job, but I had no green card yet. If the police found me working somewhere or even walking alone they could throw me in jail for being an illegal alien. They would deport me if I lived through staying in prison until they got around to sending me back; sometimes it was months before an illegal alien got to see a judge. I thought to myself, I am in prison now. Mary Belle had me work in the kitchen that day and then she asked me if I could entertain the same man again, he wanted me, I said, "I can't it's my time of the month." She became very alarmed, "Your pills, you have to take them." I said, 'It must have been when I was so sick." I acted like I was going to entertain men again, all the time making plans to get away, I pretended to eat because by now I knew there was something in the food too. I would slide my food in a napkin and pretend to swallow. They had me do laundry for a week, I stole food from the kitchen when I could and I spit out the vitamin pills. Carlotta got more and more wild. She was trying to take all the men she could to her room, everyday she looked worse; her nose was running, eyes wild, she was manic, the men did not like her looks anymore. Saturday night she came to our room and whispered one of the old men that came to see her wanted to sneak us out on Monday night. He had figured out that we could hide in his car when he went through the gate. I had already tried walking out the gate one day and found it locked and got a terrible shock just touching it. Then on Sunday, Damon came and got us and you know the rest. I still am not sure if Carlotta's dead, but I did hear a gun shot. Now, I am so worked up over Mr. Argo's talk with his sister-in-law today, no one will believe me and maybe you don't either, but I am telling the truth, how I can face people here now with two marks against me I don't know." Senna finally collapsed in tears. Chief Luis, "Whoa girl! I not only believe you. I have already heard from my friend in America that this Damon has been in trouble before. No, I believe you, but it will take time to prove all this and until then I beg you do not mention his name or anything about what happened to you, hold your head up high and know this will be solved soon."

Chief Luis was a strong looking Latino man with the typical small neat mustache and heavy dark hair cut short. He called his secretary to come get Senna's statement and type it up so Senna can sign it. He leaned back in his chair arms behind his head, "Senna do you have this Gary Valdez's phone number with you?" "Yes." Chief Luis leaned forward to his phone and called Valdez when Gary answered the Chief thanked him then asked, "I have Senna Lopez here with me. Can you give us the name and address of this—ah—I believe Clara Ring?" "Yes," Gary gave him the information and then asked if he could speak to Senna, "Senna, crying sobbed out the whole story about Mr. Argo's sister-in-law and everyone thinks she is a liar now." Gary said, "Please please don't cry. I will help the police solve this case, please can you do as the Chief says, and tell people that he has told you not to talk about it. Can you handle this alone? I am so sorry I don't know you and yet I feel I have known you all my life? Does that sound dumb to you?" "No, Senna said, I feel the same about you, thank you."

Lupe and Nika came in the room together. Nika ran to Senna and held her in her arms. Lupe with a hostile look on his face glared at Chief Luis, "My sister has been through Hell and now everyone is calling her a liar!" Chief Luis got up and shook Lupe's hand, "Lupe, I do not believe your sister is a liar, but we must be very careful, this is a powerful rich man we are after and until we have evidence we cannot catch him and you can help by making sure your sister is safe at all times and by telling people I have ordered you not to talk about any of this. Can you do that? Also, I am going to call Mr. Argo and have him call his relative back and tell her there has been a mistake and maybe Carlotta is not dead, then I will call Gonzales Police Department and give them a heads up on what to look for in their part of Mexico." Lupe smiling, "Yes, I can do all that you ask thank you."

When Lupe, Nika and Senna drove up to Maria's, Mr. Argo was sitting in a lawn chair outside. He hurried to the pickup and helped Senna out, "Please Senna, believe me I did not call you a liar. The only person I told about my phone call to Anna was Mrs. Garcia and she must have told everybody. I am so sorry Chief Luis has called me and I have done everything he asked of me. I am very worried about my niece Dahlia, but Luis said they will protect her and I am to say nothing about any of this to anyone. Your mother is furious with me she will not let me even come in the house." Senna took his hand and walked in the house where they met Maria with her arms crossed glaring at Artie. Senna said, "Ma, Chief Luis believes me and he has called Artie and asks that we all stick together and tell people the Chief has ordered us not to talk. I will just have to hold my head up and face all the gossips in this town until the law can prove me right." Senna started crying again, "No one can tell me for sure they will catch Damon Hutt, I pray to God that they do."

CHAPTER 23

Buck told Dana he was going to saddle her a horse to ride over to Billie's barbeque. "Pete and I are riding we thought you would enjoy this beautiful night." "No way, Dana said, "I'm taking your Dad's car I don't want to be gone too long. Martha will be here, but he's had a long, long day. Besides, how far is it?" "Oh, about four miles." Dana laughed, "One mile is enough for me, go you two, have fun."

When Dana went to her room to change clothes, Rosa and Mikala walked in, Mikala with her hands on her hips, "We are going to fix you up, so you're prettier than that dumb Billie. Do you have some short shorts? So everyone can see your butt cheeks." Dana collapsed on the bed laughing, "Yeah, right—no thank you—I do have some kind of short white shorts and a pink ruffled blouse. Will that do?" Mikala started fixing Dana's hair putting it up on her head with little tendrils hanging down. Mikala went through Dana's cosmetic bag dragging everything out. Serious, she said, "Stop laughing you're making your mascara run!" Dana felt uncomfortable dressing in front of two women looking her over like they were going to buy her or something. Dana looked at her legs in the mirror with the white shorts on, "I guess, I had better wear panty hose. I have varicose veins from standing on my feet for thirty years." So on went the panty hose with her anxious audience yet, she thought GOOD GRIEF! Rosa sniffed, "With the fancy people you meet tonight, they don't have veins. They don't even have red blood. I'll bet its blue too. If you sat around all day rubbing oil on your body, you would have legs like them!" Dana curious asked, "They don't work?" Rosa sniffing again, "Humph, they have all kinds of Mexicans, West's have just cattle, but the Hall's have horses and cattle and do some kind of work at home—computer work—all kinds of fancy stuff in their office. It's always locked, no one, but them can go in there. The Walkers rent out their land. They're rich from investments or something like the stock market. They have fancy horses that race and they own part of a bucking bull supposed to be making them a fortune. I miss our old neighbors. They sold out to these rich nasty people. Mrs. Halls' Mom stays there a lot and she is the best of the bunch. Now the Blair's, Mike and Amy and their girls are long time ranchers like us and they're good people." Mikala looked approval on her face, "You look beautiful. Don't let those people put you down." Troubled Dana asked, "You two really don't like these people do you?" Mikala explained, "We have to ride the bus home with their kids, Megan and Todd Hall call us "brown trash". Megan's my age and Todd is always picking on Joseph. The Walker kids sit with them and they think everything Megan and Todd do, they have to do, too." Dana was horrified, "What does the bus driver do? Are they bullies to you at school too?" Mikala said, "Oh, the bus driver tries to stop them, but he has to drive so can't see everything they do. At school they wouldn't dare mess with us. Our friends would beat them up." Dana asked, "What about the Blair's?" "Oh, Mikala said, their girls are in high school so they drive and they go up to West's to visit all the time, the girls I mean,"

CHAPTER 24

DANA WAS CAREFUL TO back Hank's fancy car out of the garage. He told her Billie West's ranch was to the right. Stay on the same road about three or four miles. You can't miss that big house its right by the road.

Dana thought about the things Rosa and Mikala had told her and she wished she had said she couldn't come, but Martha came over to stay with Hank and everybody insisted she go. As she came over a hill and around a curve she could see bright lights off to her right, the most gorgeous house, it took her breath away. Oh, my God she thought the house was built in a hill with a huge patio out front and another huge deck above it with a balcony on the second floor. The whole house looked as if it was made of glass. She turned up a circular driveway, beautiful landscaping, a huge fountain in the middle of the front yard. The lower deck was filled with people. She couldn't figure out where to park the car, when a young Latino man knocked on her car window, "Ma'am I'll take your car." Dana was so busy looking at the house she had not noticed him standing there. Mikala had insisted she wear sandals with heels, she hoped she wouldn't kill herself walking up the brick path to the patio. Billie was dressed in a long shimmering strapless gold dress, she looked like a queen. She rushed over to take Dana's hand, "Oh, you came, where's Buck and Pete?" Dana said, "They're riding over. I drove, Oh my God, Billie this is a beautiful house, Oh my!" Billie pleased laughed, "Well, we like it, come I will introduce you." Dee Hall was the first to come up, she had on a long red strapless gown, Dana thought, holy cow she's even more beautiful than Billie. Dee taking Dana's hand, "So we get to meet the miracle lady, what you did for Hank, well it's wonderful to see him out and about again, we have seen you out mowing the yard. It looks nice. Her husband, Ned came up to them and shook Dana's hand," Do you mow every day? "The people all turned to look at Dana she laughed," You mean my cowboy boots and bike shorts with a beat up farmers hat? Well, besides mowing I'm trying to start a new fashion trend." Everyone laughed. A pretty young Latino girl came to Dana and asked, "What she would like to drink?" Dana looked around and was surprised at all the young people in black and white clothes serving drinks she said, "I would have red wine if you have it?" Connie came then in a long multi-colored long gown. Dana nervous thought, boy, am I not dressed appropriate, then she looked around other women were wearing shorts and tops like Dana's. She began to relax and visited with Star Walker, who looked like a movie star, long black hair, blue eyes, like Elizabeth Taylor. Dee Hall was blond with her long hair hanging loose around her face, she looked like an angel. Star Walker introduced her children to Dana, they and the Hall children looked like little movie stars. They all asked Connie, "If they could go swimming?" "Of course," Connie said, to Dana she said—Dana, it is so nice you finally got to come to our house." Billie took Dana's hand, "Would you like to see the house?" "Yes, I would love to see your house." Dana sat her wine glass down on a round table on the patio; the tables had real flowers around vases of floating candles in water. As they entered the house she looked back and one of the children grabbed her wine and gulped it down, she was stunned, then tried to pay attention as Billie described where the rock came from for the huge fireplace that covered one whole wall. This was the family room the walls were white with shiny wood floors, a green oriental rug in the middle of the room with green striped furniture. Off the family room was a formal dining room, wood floors with a magnificent oriental rug in red and gold's under the table. Off to the left of the dining room was a formal living room done in all white and black, thick white carpet on the floor, with another huge fireplace. To the right of the dining room was a kitchen full of young and old Mexican women cooking getting things ready for dinner. The kitchen had all the most up to date equipment. There were French doors off the kitchen and dining room leading out to the pool. Off the kitchen and living room was a huge bedroom sitting room combination with a full bath, sliding glass doors led out to another small patio and the pool. Dana clapped her hands in delight, "Oh my this house is—well—just breath taking—it is beautiful!" Billie proud, "This part of the house is Aunt Eva's she can go out to the pool or sit on the patio. There was a huge stair way to the top floor where Dana had seen the balcony. There were five bedrooms each with their own bath. Billie and Connie's rooms had huge glass doors out to the balcony. The other bedrooms were for their help. Billie said, "We have a bunkhouse for the men who run the ranch. It has a big living area and everyone has their own bedroom and with a bathroom." Dana was like a little kid eyes shining "Billie, this place is so well done did you have help designing it?""Oh my, yes the middle of the house was Aunt Eva's for many years. We just gutted it out, then added on and remodeled the old house to fit in the new one. Eva stayed with us in California until the house was done. We rented an apartment; it took a year to do all this. Dana, I want to show you something, looking around like she didn't want anyone else to see." Her bedroom was pink with fancy curtains and bedspread in a pink satin. She went to her big walk in closet and brought out a dress. She held it up there was a slit clear down the middle and like holes on both sides; it was black with gold trim. Dana puzzled, "Ah, how do you hold in your top a bra would show?" Billie giggling, "It's glued on so there's just a little peek at the top." Dana felt foolish, "That looks like the movie star dresses at the awards where your—ah—tits show." Billie laughing, "That's right I'm wearing it to Buck's Stockman's convention. He told me he's not taking me, but he will change his mind after he sees this dress. Last year you ought to have seen those old biddies at the convention looking me over I thought I would really wow them this year." She sat on her bed laughing. Dana could not think of a thing to say for a minute and then, "How do the other ladies dress?" "Like old foggie long dresses, they look like peasants from the old country." She giggled again, hurrying to her closet she brought out her outfit to wear to wine tasting parties at the convention, short shorts with a halter top only partially covering her stomach. Dana laughing, "Well, I guess you will—wow-them alright—goodness you have a perfect body—not many people could wear that dress."

Going back downstairs Dana thought what a strange woman, that dress is awful! When they got back out to the patio, Buck and Pete were there. Billie grabbed Buck's arm and purred like a cat, "Let's eat big boy." Dana could see Eva and another white haired lady sitting at a table toward the back of the patio. She got another glass of wine and saying hello to all kinds of people made her way to their table. Eva took her hand and introduced her to Stella, Dee Hall's mother, Dana asked Eva all about her ranch and asked Stella, if she lived here or was just on a visit? Stella said, "I'm the kind of visitor that stays until they get tired of me. Eva's ranch foreman came with his plate full to sit with them and soon the Blair's Mike and Amy joined them. Dana told Amy, "I just about gave you a hug when I seen you were wearing shorts. I thought maybe you would think I was nuts, so I didn't —I did not expect people to be so dressed up. Amy laughed, "You know, you are like a breath of fresh air!" Stella and Dana went to get their plates—there were all kinds of wonderful food, there was a serving girl at each item on the buffet. A young Latino or Mexican man was dressed in a white uniform; he was slicing prime rib by the grill. He insisted, "He would bring Stella, Dana and Eva's steaks right to their table." Two other ranch hands joined them at the table. It was obvious to Dana that they respected and loved Eva. Russ, the foreman said to Dana, "I hear you're a miracle worker, Hanks really doing well I hear, and then laughing, I also heard you're pretty good at being a midwife for foal deliveries." Dana laughed, "That bleep, bleep mare tried to bite me and ran me out of the pen after I helped her, I gave her a long lecture on the responsibilities of motherhood. She's still mad at me today yet." Everyone at the table laughed and telling other horse stories. Dana trying to be subtle asked Eva, "Who was who again? She had met so many people at once she couldn't keep up." Eva pointed out the Halls, Walkers, and two other neighbors. Eva then pointed to several well dressed men standing together talking, "The tall man is our pilot, he is so good to us. He has business all over, but manages to stop here as often as he can." Whispering she said, "Between you and me, he is in love with Connie, but she can't see that, she is so nuts about Pete. Pete is Pete he goes from woman to woman, Connie refuses to believe this, and she thinks he is in love with her."

As the evening went on Dana's table was having a good time, the whole table roared over her blowing up a snake. Buck was sitting with Billie, but his eyes were on Dana. Billie kept touching him and trying to keep his attention on her. Dana and Amy Blair hit it off at once; they decided to get together over coffee next week, some morning over to Hanks. She said, "I heard you were fixing up the house at Hank's and the yard sure looks nice." Dana pleased, "I kind of thought maybe I was changing too much I asked Hank and he told me he was real happy with the house, it made him feel like Liz was still there." Eva sighing, "Oh, I miss Lizzy—you know Dana you remind me of her. She accepted everybody just as they were. She and Hank probably had more money than the rest of us in those days, but she never put on airs."

Amy asked Dana if Billie showed her the whole house. "Oh, yes, I am awestruck, this place is so beautiful." Amy said, "My girls would live over here if they could. They love the pool and Billie and Connie give them clothes and makeup advise. I have asked Billie if they get tired of them and she says they love having them come over it's nice to be around young people." Dana looked around at all the young girls serving. Amy seen her looking, "I know it looks like there's lots of young people all over the place, but the trouble is they don't speak English."

Dana looked at her watch, "I hate to leave, but I don't want to take advantage of Martha so I had better go. This was just wonderful, I had such a good time." Stella stood and asked, "Would you mind taking me home too? I live five miles the other way or would that be too much out of your way. I go to bed early." "Of course, I'll drive you home." Eva said, "Dana if you ever need another job where it's warm, you come take care of me." She pulled Dana down and gave her a kiss on the cheek.

Dana went over to Billie and thanked her for inviting her, she said, "I had the best time and the food was delicious. I had better go home I don't want to keep Martha out too late." Buck said, "I'm sure their alright you can stay." Billie looked at him like—shut up—and said, "Well, I'm glad you had a good time. From all the laughter at your table I could tell you were having fun." Stella went to tell Dee she was tired and she was riding home with Dana." Dee came over to Dana, "You seem to be such a nice lady, I'm glad we got to meet you and if we ever need a good nurse, we will know who to call." Dana said, "Well, thank you, that's nice to hear."

Dana and Stella chattered all the way. Stella told Dana, "Dee gets so busy with all her computer business, she don't have time to be with her children, so they need their Grandma." Dana thought back to the kid grabbing her drink and wondered what kind of mother Dee could be. She looked like she spent a lot of time on her body just like Rosa said. Stella told Dana about the time Megan and Todd was supposed to have bullied Hank's housekeeper's kids on the bus, boy, she drove in and chewed Dee up one side and down the other. Dee couldn't get a word in; she finally slammed the door in her face." Dana laughed and laughed, "You have to know Rosa—nobody—messes with her kids. They are her entire world." Stella sighed, "I wish Ned or Dee was a little more like that." Stella asked Dana in for a cup of coffee. "Well one cup, maybe then I do have to go. I guess I do want to see this house, from the road it looks really impressive, a brick house kind of in the middle of nowhere. Dana couldn't believe it possible that Dee's house was even fancier than Billie's and it even looked bigger. Two young girls were cleaning the kitchen; they stopped and poured coffee for Stella and Dana, then put out cookies that Stella had baked that day. Over coffee Stella told Dana that Dee and Ned have all kinds of young Mexican people they help to learn English and how to get green cards and jobs. "Well, Dana said, that is so nice I wish you and Dee would come over to Hank's sometime for coffee; he sleeps in the afternoon so I have time." Stella said, "I would like that, although I will be going home soon. I live in Florida, my husband don't like it here. It's too isolated. Ned and Dee have moved all over. Ned wanted to try his hand at ranching, he seems to be doing really good at it and he loves it. That's the kid's problem. They're used to private schools in Nevada." As Dana stood up, Stella said, "Are you staying on here after Hank's healed up?" "Oh no, he wants me to stay until January though and I can probably do that" Stella a sly look on her face," And Miss Dana, how about Buck, my guess he'd like you to stay a real long time." Dana rolled her eyes, "When he has something like Billie right next door —I don't —think so." Stella tapped Dana's hand, "Honey, you had better open your eyes. That man watched every move you made tonight." Dana laughed all the way out the door. On the way home she thought, DEAR GOD I could get in a lot of trouble here. What do you think? Well, it wouldn't be the first time.

CHAPTER 25

SENNA SLEPT FOR TWO days, she had wrote down everything she could think of for Chief Luis, descriptions of the people she had met and what the houses looked like, as much as she could remember.

On Friday she started her waitress job she rode with Maria in the morning. Senna loved the job even though a few people working there and customers looked embarrassed when they seen her. Maria had warned her that the small town was gossiping about her telling made up stories to make herself look good. Nika drove her home, Senna was surprised, that some tourists had left her a five dollar tip and she was grateful for Nika's support.

Sunday came way too fast for Senna, she was so nervous about meeting Gary Valdez and his family. He had called her at least once a day and sometimes twice, just to visit and he kept trying to reassure her everything would turn out alright. He said, "They would be to his Aunt Bella's Saturday night and Sunday would drive to St. Isle. They should be there by noon." Senna told him, "She had made reservations for the private dining room at the hotel and told him how to get there."

Senna did not go to church with Maria and Lupe she said, "I just can't I'm already nervous about meeting the Valdez family and I don't think I can take the stares of people who think I am a bad person and a liar."

Maria sat with Mr. Argo while Lupe went to pick up Nika, she came out all dressed up in a pink frilly dress with high heels, and Lupe could not stop looking at her, she slid across his pickup and said, "I think you maybe should watch where you're going!"

Senna put on her only nice dress, a shimmering blue sleeveless with draped material from shoulder to shoulder and a flared skirt. She put on the blue high heels that matched the dress and drove her mother's car to the hotel.

Senna Maria, Lupe, Nika and Mr. Argo sat on the chairs on the hotel porch waiting for the Valdez's. Senna could not believe her eyes when the little car she had stolen came driving up, a big white van behind it. She ran out to the little car. A tall dark handsome Latino man stepped out and hugged her; a little boy struggled out of his car seat in the back and very formal, shook Senna's hand, Senna leaned down and hugged him, then Senna put her hand on the little car's hood," This car is not just a car it is an angel from heaven." By now Maria and Lupe had met the people in the white van; Maria already had her arm around Mary pointing to Senna she said, "This is my beautiful girl Senna." Senna blushed, "Oh please, come inside." Trey looked up at her, and then took her hand. Amy, shy at first, fingers in her mouth, looked at Senna, and then took her other hand. Everyone talked at once when they got in the dining room. Senna told them, "We are going to wait for Father John. He wants to meet everybody and you must have met Father Mark Kelly, who kept the little car safe." The Valdez family laughed, "He had a huge lunch ready for us. We really enjoyed visiting with him." Senna went to get booster seats for Trey and Amy, and then she helped Mary get them settled. Father John arrived to give the blessing. Senna sat by Gary and thought, I want this moment to last forever. I don't think I've ever been this happy—it would be even better if I didn't have this black cloud hanging over my head. Gary was thinking too, God I have been sure for a week that you sent this girl to me, but I had no idea she would be so beautiful—thank you—I hope someday she will see me as more than a friend. Senna had guessed Gary would try to pay for the meal so she had made a deal in advance with Mr. Tate for her wages to go for this wonderful meal. Gary insisted on paying, but Mr. Tate would not take his money.

After the meal, the older folks sat together on the porch talking about the good old days. Lupe and Nika left so they could go to a birthday party. Barry, Nina, Gary and Senna took the children to the play ground. Nina and Senna felt like they had know each other all their lives. Senna wanted to know all about their lives in Las Vegas and

Nina was interested in Senna's life in Mexico. By 3:00 it was obvious the children were tired. Gary said, "They had better get started, they had a long drive ahead. We will probably stay in a motel in Arizona so it won't be so much driving." He asked Senna if he could speak to her alone for a few minutes, "He told her that the lead investigator on her case was a man named Patrick Dodd. What I'm going to tell you, Senna you cannot tell anyone, not even your mother." Senna close to tears, agreed. "There are now at least three agencies involved besides the local police and the Mexican police; they have found the house where you were kept a prisoner. They believe there are more like it. It snowed up at the lake so their waiting for it to melt. They want to catch everyone involved, so Damon Hutt is being followed everywhere. I will keep calling you every day." He stopped talking, embarrassed, "If you want me to keep calling." Senna took his hand," Of course, I want you to call me, I live for your calls—blushing—I'm so glad to see you in person. She touched his face, you are so handsome." Hugging her so tight she could hardly breathe he said, "And I cannot believe how beautiful you are. You have such a kind way about you, even my children trusted you right away. I wasn't going to tell you this, but I think God sent you to me." Senna stood back and looked at him, "I believe God sent you to me." They both started laughing. Gary handed her an envelope, she opened it to see a title to the little car in her name. "I cannot accept this, Oh, My God, putting her hand on her head, I already owe you so much. I will never be able to repay you." Gary said, "The car told me, it wants to be with you." Senna ran to Maria waving the paper over her head, "Gary gave me the car. Oh Mama, will it look terrible if I keep it? He says the car told him it wants to stay with me." Maria ran to Gary, "Bless you—you have done so much—how can we repay you?" Gary's mother took both Senna and Maria's hands, "Please, take the car it will make us all so happy." Senna felt sad to see the Valdez's drive off, but she was excited to now own the little car and she had hope for the future, maybe just maybe, things would get better for her.

CHAPTER 26

Monday morning Dana got Hank ready for therapy; while he shaved, she started breakfast. She could hear Sid, Buck and Hank talking while he shaved. Pete came in and said, "War party in Hank's room or what? What did you think of the party last night?" Dana said, "That was really fun. I had a good time and that house is gorgeous. I drove Dee's mother home and their house is out of this world. My goodness these people must be really, really rich." Pete said, "Everyone thought you were a character, full of fun." "Oh good," Dana said, I was nervous at all the fancy clothes, but not everyone was dressed up and I really like Amy Blair." Rosa came in then, "How was the party?" Dana laughed, "I had a good time, and Rosa I'll tell you all about it on the way to town." Buck and Sid pushing Hank's chair came out to breakfast, they all three looked at Dana. Buck said, "We need to talk to you. Rosa, can you finish breakfast?" Dana looked at them like what did I do? Buck said, "I want you to go to a stockman's convention. We fly out to California about 3:00 wednesday. That night is a banquet, on Thursday morning we have a meeting. The women can go, some go shopping or play golf, after lunch we go on a wine tasting tour. Then home Thursday night. I will get separate rooms and Sid will stay with Dad and Rosa will help too." Dana bewildered, "Oh Buck, I can't go—oh—Billie bought this—well—this fancy dress. She thinks she's going, well I can't that's all there is to it." Hank finally spoke, "Billie cost us a lot of money last year. You see, these are the people who buy our heifers and bulls. We host a two day sales event in February. We make a lot of money from this sale. We are noted for having some of the best animals around. Last year Billie created a lot of problems especially with the wives and they wouldn't come, so the men didn't come either. Buck watched how you handled people last night that you didn't know; you are perfect to heal the wounds Billie caused." Buck looked at Dana, "Please, say, yes Dana, I'll buy you anything you need and give you money to spend on whatever you want." Rosa chimed in, "You can wear one of those fancy dresses your daughter sent you. Didn't Mikala pick out one to wear to her party and that outfit you tried on Saturday would be perfect." Dana hands over her ears, "Buck, I would love to go with you, I've never been to California, but Billie will be so hurt and she will really hate me then." Buck said, "Stop this, she's lying to you. I told her two months ago long before you came along that we were never going to be together. I told her last night I was taking you, because you are good with people." Hank said, "Go! that's final." Dana looked at Rosa," Everyone will hate me if I hurt Billie." Rosa snorted, "Everyone except that Dee and the Walker woman hate Billie anyway. I told you, she's evil." Dana laughed as Rose made the sign of the cross. "Okay, I'll go. What the hell, live for the moment, right? She hugged first Hank and then Buck. Thank you both a vacation . . . yippee! Oh Rosa, can you help me with the clothes? I'm going to California. I can't believe it.

Rosa drove for the therapy session. She needed to pick up some things for Friday nights big party. Dana was sitting in the back telling them about the barbeque. Rosa looked in the rear view mirror at Dana," You went to the Halls too and you didn't see anything to make you wonder what really goes on in that house." Dana surprised, "Well, they seem to have a lot of—ah—young Mexican people working for them, but they seem to be nice to their help." Rosa gave Dana a look in the mirror that said—you're lying!

Dana was relieved when they got to town after they dropped Hank of. They went shopping to the fancy dress shop for the outfit Dana refused to buy before. She got her money out. Rosa said, "No, Mr. Buck gave me checks and told me to get you anything you wanted." On the way to the grocery store Dana said, "Don't be mad at me, Rosa, I don't know what you want from me." Rosa said "It's alright I guess I wanted something from you that you don't understand and I'm worried about you that Billie is crazy. She might try to hurt you." Dana serious, "Rosa, I just look like I'm nice. I can be real nasty if I have to and if Billie IS GOING TO TRY SOMETHING, I can handle her. In fact, I'm guessing she will be coming today. Rosa, I have to tell you about the dress." After describing the dress, Rosa and Dana laughed until tears rolled down their face. Hank was tired so they started for home right away, once again, Rosa off and on looked at Dana in the rear view mirror. Dana thought, yeah Rosa, I seen something alright, but I'm not telling you or anyone else what I think.

Rosa took lunch out to the field while Dana got Hank settled. He had a sandwich in bed, exhausted. He was soon asleep. Dana had programmed her cell number into Hank's phone, so he could push a button to get her if she was outside. She wanted to mow the ditch by the mailbox and then maybe get the fence by the barn cleaned out. Rosa went home to work on party stuff.

Dana seen the car coming and thought, Oh boy, here we go Miss Billie, I figured. Billie drove up to Dana on the mower, "I need to talk to you." Dana drove the mower up to the house while Billie waited. Dana said, "You want something to drink I'm going to have iced tea and sit on the porch." Billie red swollen eyes, "Whatever." Dana went in the kitchen, Rosa stood by the window, "I seen her drive in. I'll stay in here so you're not alone with her." Dana gave her a thumbs up, then carried two glasses of ice tea to a table. Lighting a cigarette—she said, "Okay Billie, let's get this over with." Billie's eyes were furious, "How could you worm into Bucks life so fast. Boy, you are something else. Looking straight into Billie's eyes, "Now, I'm going to tell you, what you did. You made an ass of yourself, last year at this convention. You pissed off a whole bunch of Hank and Bucks customers, so they didn't come to the annual sale, especially the women wouldn't come. That cost Hank a lot of money. Okay—the next question is about sex and no, I'm not going to sleep with Buck. You see Billie, I know better. I have dated a lot of men and it's always a mistake to mess with your boss and Buck pays my wages. Okay, the next thing you have to get through your very thick head is I'm going home to South Dakota in a month or two, then you can have Buck back with whatever relationship you have. It sounds a little strange to me. Buck insists he has told you there would never be anything between the two of you except friends. Is this true?" By now Billie was sobbing, "He just thinks he doesn't want me, I can change his mind if you will get out of the way." Dana looked at Billie, "Tell you what, I don't care one way or another so do your magic. I'm going to the convention to try to smooth over last year's disaster." Billie snorted, "Did it occur to you it wasn't me that lost customers maybe the Bolts' livestock did not meet up with the customers' expectations?" Dana laughed, "That might be the case, it doesn't matter. They have asked me to go and I'm going to do my best to make nice. They have been good to me. One more thing I doubt Billie that I'm the kind of playmate that could keep Buck happy. I'm only guessing here, I kind of think men can be—well—like tom cats, checking out any new thing that comes along in their territory." Billie looked at Dana then laughed, "You know I like you, you're a lot smarter than I gave you credit for. You're right, I'm going home and set a trap for a tom cat and I have (shaking her body) the right kind of bait." She waved as she drove off.

Dana in the house could hear Rosa giving Hank the whole conversation. Dana stood in the doorway; Hank looked at her, his eyes twinkling. Rosa was furious; she turned to Dana, "Stand by your man!" Hank and Dana both laughed, Dana said, "He's not my man. In my lifetime, I have never met a man worth fighting for. If I can't hold onto one without a fight, I don't want him."

Later Hank and Dana were sitting on the porch having their evening smoke and cocktail, Dana heard the men come home. Buck stomped out on the porch, "So I'm a tom cat. What the hell made you say that, and I never met a man worth fighting for, what the hell—and what's this about playmates? I did get busy and forgot to call about another room Wednesday night, so I suppose I had better get that done—RIGHT AWAY." Dana calm, "Rosa called you? This room has two beds—right?" Buck disgusted running his hands through his hair, "Yes it does, what next?" Dana said, "Well, I think we can stay in one room. After all we sleep across the hall from each other now and I don't see any worn spots on the floor and you can't tell me a man who's been divorced for some twelve or so years has not had a few playmates." Buck beat his head on the porch door, "I guess if you say so." "I did the tom cat thing so Billie left with some dignity. What should I have done—beat her up?—pull her hair?—and maybe you are a tom cat. How do I know?" Dana thinking it over when and put her arms around him, "You know, I probably got carried away. I'm sorry, I want us to go to California and live it up for two days, like a mini vacation." Buck finally started laughing. Dana said, "Rosa, you can come out now. I made a big pot roast in the crock pot and I made sour cream raisin pie. You can help me throw some plates on let's eat." Sid playfully punched Pete and went —MEOW—They had a good time teasing Buck. Sid admitted he was off to El Paso again, he gave Dana a hug, "I'm not being a tom cat, honest, I really—really—like Lucia." Dana laughed, "I know you do. I seen the way you looked at her the first day you met, you're a good man."

Later Dana and Bo dog settled on Dana's little patio, Buck came out and joined them. He was quiet at first. Dana told him, "Hey, handsome man. I've had a few playmates too."

CHAPTER 27

TUESDAY MORNING DANA WAS fixing breakfast when she heard another conference in Hank's bedroom, now what, she thought. When everyone settled at the table—Sid told her, "Dana, when I go to visit Lucia she has me park three houses down and then walk across the neighbors yards. That's how they get home because they are sure this man is having them watched." Dana shocked sat down, "Dear God, her mother told me they were like prisoners in their own home. Oh, my God that's awful. Are they being paranoid or is this true?" Sid sighed, "The neighbors are all on alert and they think someone working for him rented an apartment down the street—they can't prove it, but with binoculars he could see everything they are doing. What I want to do is move Lucia and the kids to my house in Sunbird. It's not very clean right now, but it can be fixed up. Dad and Grandpa agreed—I want her to put Josh in school in Sunbird with a different name and believe or not her Dad wants her to do it. He's going to set it up with the school. I don't want anyone to think—ah—well, that I'm taking advantage of some poor mixed up girl." Dana hugged him, Sid take advantage, who cares, as long as you can keep that girl and those kids safe. If you would have seen that horrible Father and how scared those kids were. Well, it was awful." Sid hugged her back, "One more thing, I want to sneak her and the kids out tonight, to stay here on the ranch, until we can get the house in town fixed up. I was wondering if you could clean two of the bedrooms upstairs and well—kind of fix them up.?" Dana clapped her hands dancing around, "You have made me a happy woman. I love Lucia and I have tried to think of a way to help her, you are a life saver. Of course, I'll fix up some rooms right after breakfast."

Hank told Dana, "You know, one of the rooms upstairs was pink with frilly stuff all over, my daughter's room, the other room with the bunk beds had superman stuff for Sid. I think you might find the storage room upstairs full of stuff for those rooms. Rosa cleans those rooms up when my daughter comes, but she puts everything away after they leave—she hates messing with, what she calls fussy stuff."

Dana hurried through the mornings work so she could get upstairs. The beds and windows were bare. She started out washing the windows, wiping down the walls. She sprayed the mattresses and washed and waxed what turned out to be beautiful wood floors. While the floors dried she was ready to check out the storage room. There was almost new everything for the pink room, ruffled pink flowered curtains, and matching sheets and bedspread. There was a large pink rug for the middle of the room—two pink upholstered chairs—even pictures to hang on the wall —the nails still there. She found a night stand with a pink ruffled lamp. Dana was having the time of her life, when she remembered Rosa was busy so she was taking lunch out to the men who were fixing fence, somewhere north of the ranch. She made sandwiches, chips, cake, and coffee. She took the old pickup sitting in the yard. She thought this is fun—she kept driving for what seemed miles when she found them. Buck came up as she was setting lunch up on the tailgate, "You drove this pickup, you can drive a stick shift?" Dana surprised, "Sure, I can drive about anything that has wheels." Manuel told Dana, "Rosa called him and told him about Lucia coming, Rosa wanted Dana to call her if she needed help." Dana said, "I am having a blast, I love playing house fixing rooms up, I am about done."

Dana drove home and got Hank up for his dinner. He managed to walk with his walker to the table. Dana was thrilled. He told her he would sit up a while so go ahead with her project. She found the Superman curtains, sheets and bedspreads for the bunk bed room; it also had a single twin bed on the other wall, there was a bright blue rug for the middle of this room too. Rosa had picked the kids up from school. They all trooped upstairs and oohed and awed over how pretty it looked. Dana thought when they leave, I'm going to wash and wax this whole hallway. I'll bet there's beautiful wood underneath all this ground in dirt. Hank had cookies and milk with the kids, then he went off to bed and Rosa and the children went home. Dana did get everything done and loved the shiny floors.

That night Dana served frozen pizzas, no time to cook, but she was satisfied with all her work. Buck, Dana and Hank sat on the porch waiting for Sid. It was really late when he drove up with his little family. Dana hugged everybody; the kids were excited to be on the ranch. Dana was so proud to show them their rooms; they were thrilled, looking at everything. Dana felt like they were her grandchildren, she was as excited as they were. Lucia helped put Hank to bed so she could help him while Dana was gone.

CHAPTER 28

WEDNESDAY MORNING DANA DROVE Hank to therapy for the first time by herself. He used his walker to walk in the clinic. She went to pick up some convenience foods for Lucia to make. When they got home Hank went right to bed. Dana had laid out her clothes the night before to take to California. She was excited as she carefully packed everything in one bag. Dana was going to take her time getting dressed. She put on white western cut pants and a black fringed western blouse with silver buttons holding the fringe, then she struggled with the fancy wide western belt with a big silver buckle, Rosa insisted she buy. Buck was ready. He came to get her suitcase and stopped dead in his tracks, when he saw her outfit, he whistled, "You look like a cowgirl movie star." Dana laughed, "Well, you bought the belt."

Driving off the two of them was like two little kids going to Disney World. On the plane Dana read a goofy book out loud to Buck. At the airport on arrival there was a limousine from the hotel waiting for them. Dana was nearly hanging out the window looking at everything. They had to hurry after they got to their room because the banquet started at 6:30. Buck dressed first in the bathroom. When he came out he mixed them both a drink to fortify them, he said. Dana came out of the bathroom with a red dress, sleeveless with one side over her shoulder and a long straight skirt with a slit up the side. Her hands were shaking as Buck watched her put her hair up on her head and the extra eye liner. Finally she added all the rhinestone jewelry she owned, long sparkling earrings and a huge bracelet. Through all this Buck watched in amazement, she finally twirled around, "So, cowboy what do you think?" He was speechless, "You are like some kind of

chameleon, every time I look at you—you are more beautiful, wow!"
He handed her a drink she said, "I'd better have a strong snort before
I meet all these people, I'm a little nervous." Buck put his drink down,
then put hers down. He pulled her tight to him he said, "So I'm a
tom cat, I can't help it—you are the most amazing woman—no matter
what you are doing—I've never felt this way about any woman before
and, of course—I know you absolutely will not believe me." Dana
touched his face then kissed him, "I do believe you, now, let's go see
how we do in the world outside the ranch." Just before they went out
the door Dana stopped shocked, "My God, Buck, I'm sorry I was so
busy worrying how I looked I didn't notice your clothes." He had on a
black western fitted suit that must have cost a fortune. His boots were
of the best leather, there were gold rings on his hands. His gold string
tie and black hat were not cheap. Dana now really nervous, "You are so
handsome and expensive looking, while everything I have on is fake."
Buck took her hand, "There's nothing fake about you and you look
fine."

They were seated at a table with three other couples. Buck knew
all of them and introduced Dana as his Girl, Friday, who takes care of
everyone on the ranch. They all asked about Hank. Buck pointed to
Dana, our miracle worker; she has him back on his feet. The food was
delicious and Dana always interested in the people around her soon
was the life of the party. After dinner they were invited to the lounge
for drinks and dancing. Dana met two of the older woman in the
ladies room. They said, "They heard she was the best nurse anybody
could possibly ask for and she was from South Dakota." One of them
asked, "Do you play golf in South Dakota?" Dana laughed, "Oh yes,
we are really a tourist state so there are many country clubs and really
fancy golf courses, I play, but not very good, but I love trying." Both
women said, "Oh, good we are short of a player this year. Would you
like to join us? That would make eight of us, two groups; we play in
the morning early because it gets so hot here, let's say about 7:30,
the hotel has a breakfast buffet, we will meet you there. Do you have
clothes along to play?" Dana said, "I have everything but, a visor hat."
"No problem one said, I will bring you one of mine."

Eleven o'clock that evening found Dana and Buck sitting with
several young couples. Buck and Dana got up to dance he said, "I'm
so proud of you." Dana whispered, "I was going to tell you the same

thing, these people really respect you." When they sat down at the table one of the men said, "Let's go down the street to that crazy lounge, anybody up for that?" A lot of people had left the lounge area after the banquet. Buck asked Dana, "Should we go to a wild party place?" "Sure—she said, the only thing is I have to get up early to have breakfast because Mildred and Tilly are picking me up at 7:30 to play golf." The whole group at the table stopped talking, "What did you say? They asked you to play golf, how in the world did you meet them?" One of the women held her fingers up with air quotes, "You have been inducted into the elite club of the richest of the rich people." Dana flabbergasted looking at Buck, "I met them in the ladies room—why—doesn't everybody play golf? I told them I'm not very good, but they said they needed another player." She looked around her at the silent group, "What?" Everyone laughed, "Girl you had better be on your best behavior with those old girls." Dana went, "Humph, "They will have to accept me as I am." Someone else said, "Maybe they want a nurse with them in case one of them passes out from being uptight." Dana looked anxious at Buck for a minute than burst out laughing. They all climbed in two cabs and went to the wild place. Dana took off her high heels and danced up a storm, she was having so much fun, and other people came to join them. She asked Buck what time it was, "He said like 2:00 in the morning—should we go?" "Yeah I guess, I'm having so much fun though I hate for the night to end, she hugged everybody goodbye, then wrote down their cell numbers in case she got dumped from the golfers, she could go shopping with them." When they got up to leave some of the men yelled out, "I'll bet there will be a hot time in room 302 tonight." Dana rolled her eyes, "Yeah—right—I am totally blitzed—I drank enough tonight for three people. I'll be lucky if I don't have to crawl on my hands and knees to room 302." Buck and Dana took a cab. They had the driver go through a drive through sandwich shop. They took coffee and food back to the hotel.

When they got back to their room, Buck went in the bathroom and came out with Black Angus bulls all over his pajamas, Dana collapsed laughing. She came out in her old soft pajamas, jumped on his bed gave him a kiss then jumped on her bed and under the covers. "Thank you, Buck. I had the best time tonight. Maybe the best time of my whole life." And she was out.

Dana was up and dressed by 6:30 A.M., she put her hair in a pony tail—on went the panty hose with the white shorts and ruffled blouse, with her nurse shoes to complete the outfit.

Buck woke up at 7:30 and seen she was gone. Dana took her time eating breakfast, true to their word the older women came in and sat with her. A hotel van drove them to the golf course. Dana had the time of her life with the old women and to her surprise she played alright. They finished up nine holes then went into the fancy Country Club Lounge. Dana about fainted when they all ordered beer, she thought what the heck that sounds good. I'm probably still drunk from last night. I might as well keep on. Mildred asked her, "What happened to the blonde bombshell Buck had been seeing." Dana, "Ah—well—Buck got rid of her I think." The women laughed when Mildred said, "He would have to kill that woman to get rid of her." Riding back in the hotel van, Dana asked, "What she should she wear for the wine tasting. Were they dressing up?" Tillie said, "It's not real formal, we will be having lunch at the Country Club though and it's pretty fancy" They all went to their rooms.

Dana took her time showering, fixing her hair and dressing up in her new outfit, she left her hair down. Buck came in at noon; he was dressed in dress western slacks and a white shirt. Once again, they had to hurry to catch the hotel van for a ride to the very exclusive Country Club. Mildred and Tillie called them over to their table, "You look good, is this outfit fake too?" Then they laughed, "Sit with us.' Buck squeezed her arm and pulled out her chair. The old ladies told him how much fun it was to golf with Dana, "It's not too often we get to play with an enthusiastic golfer that jump up and down cheering when they make par." Buck looked at Dana, "You?"

After lunch the winery van drove them from one beautiful home to another even more fabulous. While the others toured the winery itself, Dana would be invited in to see the houses. She was thrilled to be included with the young women more interested in home decorating than wine making.

It was late afternoon when tired—full of wine—with more wine bottles in their hands—everyone said goodbye—many hugs and exchanged phone numbers later, found Buck and Dana back on a plane headed for home. When they got settled Buck holding Dana's hand leaned over and whispered, "How did you—get in with the rich crowd?" Dana, "Oh, oh, you figured it out—well—I looked for the people who wore simple comfortable clothes. Very rich people are far more interested in spending money on something that brings back money and that's not clothes, so when I seen those particular kind of women go to the ladies room, I followed. I stood at the sink washing my hands, I asked them where they came from and stuff like that. The one told me I had a beautiful dress on. I said, 'Well, to tell you the truth, I paid fifty dollars for this dress at Penney's, the jewelry I bought at a pawn shop, so you might say everything I have on is fake." The whole bathroom laughed, "They asked about your Dad and I said, "I was his nurse and he was giving me a two day vacation with his handsome son. That's when they asked me if I played golf." Buck just shook his head and they both fell asleep.

When they got off the plane they went to eat in a restaurant in El Paso, they talked and talked. Sid and Lucia were waiting up for them when they got home. Hank was in bed and so were the kids. Lucia said, "They wanted to stay up to see you, but couldn't keep their eyes open. Dana you sleep in—in the morning I'll make breakfast." Dana said, "May God Bless you." Hank called out from the bedroom to her, "Did you have a good time?" I loved it. I don't think I have ever had that much fun. I think I might still be drunk. I'll tell you all about it in the morning." Dana fell into bed with her clothes on.

CHAPTER 29

THURSDAY MORNING GARY VALDEZ's secretary rang him, "You have an emergency call." Scared he picked up. It was Clara Ring she said, "Gary, I know I shouldn't call you at work, but this is important. That FBI guy that talked to me, brought some men with dogs here to the park this morning. They must have found something because now there are all kinds of police cars, ambulances, hearses and two coroner vans. We think they are by the old well that's up there. We forgot all about it. I thought it had been filled in years ago—anyway Dad and I are packing up—well, we're scared—we are headed for our daughter's. Can you call that poor girl—Senna—and tell her she is not a liar—something really bad happened up here." Gary stopped Clara interrupting, "Clara would Damon Hutt know who your daughter married?' Clara said, "I guess he could, I don't know." Gary said, "I think Clara you should go to my house or I forgot Mom's home alone with the kids, better yet, go to Barry's house. Damon don't know Barry, he does know me, Nina's home all day, yes, I will call Nina, do you have a cell?" "Yes, Gary I'm glad you thought of Nina. No one is going to mess with her. Yes, we will call her when we get to town. Here's our number and I will write down her number."

When Clara hung up Gary called his mother and Nina and gave them a heads up on the situation. He decided to tell them that he handled Damon's account and the IRS was in the office right now. He told his mother, "Ma, maybe you should take the kids and go to Nina's, too. She is darn tough, I know she can handle just about anything that comes along." Mary agreed.

Senna was at work when Mr. Tate came up to her and said, "A Gary Valdez wants you to call him as soon as possible, at this number, it sounded important." Senna did have a break coming so she went outside and called the number Gary answered on the first ring, "Oh, thank God, you called, remember Mrs. Ring from the lake, well she just called me the police brought dogs up to the park this morning. Senna, can I call you right back, can you wait?" Gary went outside and stood behind a tree to call Senna back, "Senna—Oh, God—How can I tell you this, there are all kinds of police cars, hearses and coroner vans up there." Senna could not speak. Gary said, "'Senna did you hear me?" She finally spoke barely a whisper, "Oh, my God, Gary, it's true, there must be more than Carlotta. Oh, my God, oh, my God, she was trying to talk through tears." Gary said, "The Rings are scared so they're going to my brother's house, so is my mother and children and what I'm not supposed to tell you, the IRS is here at my office with a subpoena for all Damon Hutt's business deals. I have spent all morning answering their questions, please don't tell anyone, but I thought you deserved to know, after the hell this man put you through. I'll call you as soon as I get home—ah—I love you." Senna stood staring at the phone in her hand. In her heart she knew it was all true, but her mind could not accept it. Then it dawned on her Gary said "I love you." She looked up to see Father John and Chief Luis getting out of a police car. They both looked at the tears running down her face. Father John holding her hand, "You know?" She shook her head, yes. Chief Luis asked if her mother was working today. Once again Senna shook her head, yes. Father John and Senna sat on a bench she stared straight ahead. Neither of them said a word. Chief Luis came out with Maria, she was holding her purse—crying—she said, "Senna, I must go to Mr. Argo's. Oh, Senna you were right. They think they have found Carlotta." Chief Luis took both of Senna's hands, "Without your help and your courage, Senna, this man would have got away with murder. Now, I don't want you to go home because Damon Hutt flew his plane off yesterday, we know where it's at, but we want to catch more of the people involved. You are to stay at Father John's. Do you understand how serious this is?" Senna nodded—yes.

Mr. Tate told Senna to leave for the rest of the day and she asked if she could stay, "I'll be alright in a minute, I am having trouble believing all the terrible things that have happened—it's like a bad nightmare—only it's real."

When Mr. Argo came out of his barn to see the police car, he put his hands over his eyes. "Chief Luis, Father, Maria, I don't want to know why you're here." Maria took him in her arms and they all went in the house Maria made coffee. Chief Luis explained what he knew. He told Mr. Argo that he would have to go to a Las Vegas morgue to identify Carlotta and there was always the chance that it's not her, "Is there something we can we can help you do or do you have enough money?" Mr. Argo wiping his face, "Money is not a problem, but Maria do you have a passport?" Maria surprised, "Oh no, I have never been anywhere besides—well—maybe fifty miles from home." Mr. Argo turned to Chief Luis, "Please, could you arrange a way for her to go with me? Maybe—I don't know—maybe fly out of Tucson. Yes, that is what we will do is drive to Tucson, then fly from there." Father John said, "I will drive you to Tucson and visit my old friend Father Mark, while you're gone, he can drive you to the airport." Chief Luis said, "I will get Maria cleared." Maria said, "You know Artie, Mrs. Valdez invited us anytime to come stay with her in Las Vegas. I can have Senna call her, will that be alright?" "Yes," Mr. Argo then thanked the Chief and Father John for coming. Father John said, "I can get plane tickets pretty cheap, would you want me to do that? I will get them right away come to my house when you get some things together and I will be ready."

Senna called Gary at work again, "Gary, I'm so sorry to call you at work. Is it possible for you to help Mr. Argo and my mother, Chief Luis came and said they need to fly to Las Vegas to identify Carlotta—even though it might not be her. I don't know, I feel so awful." Gary interrupted her, "I will take care of them, I am happy to help any way that I can, I will pick them up from the airport and take them to my house. I will drive them where ever they need to go—I will take care of them don't you worry. Is there any way you could come too, I would buy your ticket?" Senna crying again, "I can't, I want to come so bad, but Mr. Tate without Mama and one of the other girls cut her hand—I have to stay—he has been so good to me." Gary told her, "You are right. He will need your help, this news will hit the papers soon and you will have lots of people there. Take care of yourself and have your mother call my cell when they find out their flight and the time." Mr. Argo threw a few clothes in a duffle bag and dressed in his nicest suit. Maria had ridden back to her house with

Chief Luis; she was excited and scared at the same time. She drug out an old suitcase, and changed into her one really nice suit. By the time she had packed a few extra clothes, Mr. Argo was driving in. He said, "Maria what would I do without you?" He carried out her suitcase and they hurried to Father John's, Chief Luis was there with a pass for Maria. Father John already had his car out—he, too was sad, but excited to go visiting, too. He had called Father Mark to get the tickets and he was happy to find out Mr. Argo had bought a cell phone. Father Mark called them and said, "You probably should hurry, I found two cheap round trip tickets from 6:00 p.m. tonight, then return at noon the next day. I hope that will give you enough time."

Father Mark's housekeeper had made lunch for them that was like a full meal. They made it to the airport early. Maria and Artie clung to each other as the plane took off. They were terrified, but by the time they arrived in Las Vegas they had kind of settled down. Gary Valdez was waiting for them. Maria kissed him. He told them, "They would be going to his brother's house for supper, but they would be staying at his house overnight. Nina and Mary had wonderful food laid out, Maria told them, "Father Mark's housekeeper had a huge lunch for us, but we were so nervous on the plane. Food sounds good again." Clara, Mary and Maria sat and talked and talked, they hashed over Clara's story and Senna's story too. Maria and Artie were in awe over Nina's beautiful house. Clara Ring's daughter stopped in too, she was checking on her parents, so she had more of the story, how mean Damon used to be. Every one assured them they would pray for them the next day and would meet Artie and Maria when they got done with this awful ordeal.

Gary took Artie, Maria and his mother home with him. The Ring's stayed at Barry's house—Gary left the children with Nina's girls everyone thought that was safer.

Artie stayed up all night at various times Gary, Maria or Mary sat with him, he was terrified of what the next morning would bring.

The next morning Gary picked up his Priest to go with them to the morgue that seemed to help Artie.

CHAPTER 30

SENNA COULD NOT KEEP up with the rush of curious people that came to the restaurant, some hugged her, all sat down for coffee or sweet rolls some had hamburgers. Senna tried to be friendly, but she could not forget how these same people had been so willing to think bad of her, now they were falling all over her especially wanting to hear some new gossip. Mr. and Mrs. Tate had to help with the crowd so Senna kept on working into the night shift. She told them she wanted to be busy so she didn't have time to think. At closing time Mrs. Tate followed Senna's little car to Father John's house to make sure she was safe. Myra was still there and Lupe and Nika came over. Senna was exhausted, but knew she probably could not sleep. Chief Luis called her and asked for a description of the clothes Carlotta had on that last time she seen her. Senna said, "I can describe every detail to you that day will be in my mind until the day I die." Senna started sobbing again after she hung up, Myra said, "Senna, STOP THIS, you know you must not do this, you are feeling guilty that Carlotta's dead and your alive. God saved you for a purpose just as he will use Carlotta's death to bring about good. Someone needed to stop this evil man." Senna looked at Myra, "Your right, I vowed I would get him some day, and I hope the police can catch him, I hope he has not found out their looking for him. Chief Luis said the Las Vegas police was going to try to keep it out of the news until they were ready to reel him in, that how he described it to me." Gary called Senna then and she told him all the worries on her mind, shyly she said, "I thank God every day that I stole your car, how else would I have met you."

CHAPTER 31

GARY WAS DETERMINED TO try to help Artie get through this; Gary's priest was a kind man, who prayed with all of them in the car. Patrick Dodd and other police were waiting for them. He shook Artie's hand and patted Maria on the back saying, "I'm sorry you have to go through this, there are five other families suffering today too." The coroner said they would be viewing the body through a window. When he opened the curtains Artie took one look and collapsed. Patrick Dodd and Gary helped him to a chair. Maria was so stunned she kept looking at Carlotta. It was definitely Carlotta, she thought she would look terrible; instead she was all cleaned up and looked like she was sleeping. Puzzled she asked Gary, "There's not a mark on her!" Mr. Dodd came to Maria, "We will talk over here so sometime Mr. Argo will want to know, just not today, she was shot behind her ear and then wrapped in a blanket. We sent your daughter a picture of it and she identified it as the one Damon had used." Maria quietly cried then asked, "What's next? How do we get our girl home?" Several people helped make the necessary arrangements. Artie gave Gary a check to pay for what was needed.

When they left Artie told them, "I think I have held my breath for —what—many days hoping, but somehow I knew she was dead. I'm relieved in a way to have the wondering over and I know where she's at."

All the Valdez's and the Rings met Gary, Artie and Maria for brunch in a nice restaurant. At the airport everyone was crying. Maria looked up to see Gary rolling a suitcase up to them. Mr. Argo arms in the air clapping, "You are going with us, oh God Bless You—here—I will pay for your ticket. Maria and I was so afraid flying here." Gary said, "I bought the ticket yesterday. I had a feeling the trip home might be rough for both of you and I'm sure you can guess by now I want to be with Senna." Maria patted his hand, "She told me she thinks God sent you to her. I believe she is right. How else would the two of you have met?" Gary threw back his head and laughed, "I am positive God was behind this, I have been so lonely since my wife died sometimes depressed is this all there is to life? Working and raising my children, that should be enough, but I need a partner."

Father John sunburned from playing golf, was sad to hear about Carlotta, but secretly happy to have had this little vacation. He was relieved to have Gary drive home.

Senna was working extra hours in the restaurant again because it seemed the town people wanted to gather some place together, to share their grief over Carlotta. She was cleaning off a table when she looked up to see Gary Valdez leaning against the counter. She rubbed her eyes like she was seeing things then ran straight into his arms. He waited while she finished cleaning up. He said, "I left my suit case at Father John's." Senna said, "You are staying at my house."

It wasn't until Saturday morning Mr. Argo remembered his niece, Dahlia, she was with Damon Hutt, He had Maria help him explain to Anna Gonzales about Carlotta and Senna's narrow escape from death. Anna started screaming, "Oh, My God, Artie what do I do? Dahlia calls every Saturday night about 7:00. I can't call her because the woman she's staying with don't want them to have cell phones and that made Dahlia suspicious so she hides her phone. What am I to do?" Maria told her, "I will call Chief Luis here and have him call you. All he has told us is that they have this Damon under surveillance, but their waiting for a search warrant from some Judge." Maria called Chief Luis and told him about this new mess he said, "I will handle it don't worry. We are closing in on him."

CHAPTER 32

DANA DID SLEEP IN Friday morning. When she sat up in bed, three little boys rushed in her room to tell her all about the ranch and their Grandma was coming with Carmen to clean their new house today and they get to go to a party tonight, Mikala invited them and Grandma was coming to the party, too. Dana laughed at the excited faces she said, "Guess what? We all get to dance too."

Dana found Hank outside on the porch she flustered said, "I almost forgot it's therapy day. Why didn't you wake me up?" He laughed, "I changed the appointment to a later time. I told them my nurse had a hangover. We have plenty of time. I heard some excited kids getting you up. Lucia's washing some clothes then she's going to work on the house in town."

Hank's therapy went really good so he was graduated to a walker. He looked so proud walking to the car. Dana and Hank went to the lounge for lunch. Hank enjoyed showing off his walker to his old pals. After lunch they went to see Sid's house. Dana laughed and laughed, "When Lucia's mother told her how her housekeeper drove her own car here, in town—Lucia's mother had laid down in the front seat.

She said this cloak and dagger stuff was maybe not necessary, better save then sorry. We brought some dress up clothes for all of us to go tonight—Rosa is so busy, but still took time to bring us lunch and she called me yesterday and invited us to Mikala's party. Dana, Lucia tells me if it hadn't been for you grabbing Joey away from Richard, he would have been stronger than Lucia. She would have had to go back with him, she would never have left her child behind. Don and I don't know how we can ever repay you." If Dana could have looked in the future she would have seen she would desperately need a lawyer.

CHAPTER 33

EVERYONE WAS DRESSING AT the ranch even though there were three bathrooms. It was still like a zoo. The ceremony at the church would start at 5:00 p.m., then on to the reception and dance in the VFW Hall. When Dana came out in her red long dress with all the sparkly jewelry, everyone stopped talking. Sid whistled. Hank said, "Let's get a picture, our nurse has turned into Cinderella, my God girl, you are beautiful." Buck kept on smiling. While he took her picture he said, "She cleans up good" As he took her hand, "Madame, I will be escorting you tonight—well—I am also your driver". Dad thinks we need a chaperone so he is taking Martha and going with us. I'm not sure who needs a chaperone though." Sid was driving Lucia, her mother, Carmen, and the children.

When they got to the church Lucia sat by Dana so she could explain the ceremony. Dana curious as always, watched everything. When Mikala and her young man walked down the aisle with Manuel following, Dana wanted to clap, and Mikala was stunning in her fancy dress. Dana whispered to Lucia, "What's with the shoes Manuel is carrying?" Lucia explained, "The father helps his daughter step into fancy high heels." Dana was fascinated with all the rituals and the soaring Spanish music. When they left the church Buck was holding Dana's hand. He looked so proud to be with Dana. She was too busy hugging and talking to people she didn't notice. Martha drove Hank to the reception while most of the crowd walked. They looked like an Easter parade with all the bright colorful long gowns. Rosa cheeks were flushed. She was gorgeous in a long black and white dress with a flared skirt. Lucia was in a peach strapless gown that showed off her black hair and beautiful bronze skin. She fit in with the Mexican people instantly. Although Mikala truly did out shine them all with her happy gleaming face and her dress was exquisite.

There was a long table covered with food, all kinds of Mexican cuisine. Dana was going to try a little of everything, the too spicy stuff, she was careful to take a small amount. The wine was served in plastic wine glasses each with a bow tied on the stem and down the middle of each table a streamer of colorful flowers ran the length of the table. Later the streamers would be hooked into necklaces for everyone. There were candles everywhere and little lights all across the ceiling with what looked like real stars flashing on the ceiling too. The tables were cleared out after the meal and the dancing began with Mikala and Manuel first and then Mikala and her grandfathers. Buck and Dana sat with Hank, Martha and Mike and Amy Blair. Sid brought his new family over to sit after he had proudly introduced them to everyone in the hall. When Buck and Dana got up to dance there were several whistles and cat calls, everyone teasing them. After they danced a fast polka someone yelled out to Buck—you had better keep that nurse—in case, you have a heart attack. Hank told Sid he was getting tired, Lucia's mother and Carmen said, "They were ready to go, too." Dana said, "Oh, we can go." "No", Sid said, "I'll drive them home and then come back. Lucia's going to do some kind of traditional round dance and I don't know the first thing about it so I have an excuse not to participate." Lucia and the children were having a blast. A lot of the young people lined up for a special Mexican dance. Lucia fit right in, Dana felt so happy she thought this town and its people have already accepted Lucia. She will be safe here, they must know her story, and they will protect her that was obvious. Buck, Dana and the Blair's went outside; Dana took her glass of wine and lit up a cigarette. The West's were sitting at a picnic table outside the lounge, the Halls and Walker's were sitting with them also Billie's pilot with his friends. They called Buck and Dana over, Billie said, "Well, nurse you look pretty good." Dana laughed, "I doubt I can fix up as good as you can—you look beautiful always and I—well—some days I look like something the cat drug in." Everyone laughed. Buck put his arm around Dana then and said, "She's a cheap date. She loves this cheap wine they're serving." Dana laughed, "I'm probably going to get shit faced, but this wine tastes good to me." Buck and the Blair's told the barmaid to bring them some tap beers, we could live without the wine.

Pete was sitting with Connie, but he stood up and said, "Dana, I hear them playing some salsa music. Do you want to try one dance and see if you can keep up?" Dana waved goodbye and bounced off with Pete. She thought I'll probably make a fool of myself, but so what, live for the moment—right? When Buck came in, he watched Pete and Dana. They looked pretty good. Dana laughing came and put her arm around Buck, "Thank you Pete. That was fun." Buck and Dana did a slow dance, then he staggered, Dana alarmed, "What's wrong?" He said, "I feel funny. Let's sit down." He was white and sweating, Dana took his pulse, "Your heartbeat seems slow. Are you sick to your stomach?" Mike said, "Oh, I bet it's the flu. I had it last week and I thought I was going to die." Buck looked terrible Dana said, "We're going home I'll have Sid take us." Amy Blair said, "We're ready to go. We'll take you home, it's right on the way." While Buck drank some ice water, Dana went to tell Rosa and Manuel that Buck had the flu so they were leaving. She told them what a good time she had and the food was out of this world.

On the way home Buck looked like he was passed out. Dana invited the Blair's to come in, but they said, "Some other time when Buck felt better." Buck staggered and needed Dana's help to get to his bed, she got his jacket, boots and belt off. He held on to the sheet, "The rooms going around it's spinning," Then he seemed to fall to sleep, breathing normal. Dana went to her room to change clothes and get some pajamas on, when she heard Buck giggling. She ran to his room. He looked up at her, "How did we get home?" Dana took his vital signs again. Hank hollered, "What's going on?" Dana, "I don't know. Buck got sick at the dance." "Did he drink too much or what?' "No, I drank more than he did and he's acting funny. I'm not going to wait too long before I take him to town to the emergency room." Sid and Lucia came in, "Is Dad alright?" Dana puzzled, "I don't know he's really out of it. Mike Blair said he had a flu like this. I checked his pulse and blood pressure that seems fine." Buck started mumbling, laughing a silly look on his face, but not moving. She told Sid, "If I didn't know better I would think he was on some kind of drug." Sid asked her, "Do you want me to stay here with you?" By then Buck had fallen back to sleep. Dana, "I'll call you if he gets any worse." Dana sat in a chair and was about asleep when Buck started shivering. She climbed in bed with him and held him and he went back to sleep. She was replaying the conversation with Billie and it occurred to her that Billie might have slipped him something in his beer. She probably planned on getting Dana, but she had held her wine glass in her hand. Buck woke up some time later, "I'm going to be sick, help me to the bathroom quick." He was terrible sick, but thought he felt better. Dana helped him back to bed and he started shivering again. She held him tight, then he started breathing normal and seemed to be fine. When she woke up it was morning and she had her legs and arms around Buck—and—the whole family was standing by the bed staring at her. Buck woke up bewildered he grabbed Dana, "You slept with me and I don't remember anything." Everyone laughed. Dana got up dressed and helped Hank button his shirt, then she started breakfast. When Buck came out he still looked tough, puzzled, he shook his head, "I can't remember a thing after we danced a slow dance. What is going on?" Rosa came in she took one look at Buck and said, "I seen you outside last night by Billie, I'll bet she put something in your drink." Buck snorted, "No, for God's sake. I have the flu, ask Dana she had to help me all night. Did you have to help me to the bathroom?" Frowning at Dana, "Yeah, she said and that was sooooo romantic, why we had the time of our life." For a minute Buck looked horrified and then he said, "I never know if you're kidding or—not." Lucia and family came down to breakfast, Lucia said, "I think we can stay at our house tonight. There's enough furniture and Mom brought new bedding. Sid and Buck, when you get done with your meeting tonight stop in, I'll show you the house. I think it looks pretty good." Buck told her we will do that if it doesn't get too late. I'm still not feeling the best. Dana said, "I forgot you guys have a stockman's meeting tonight." Buck said, "Manuel's going too. I'm giving a talk about the convention and what new stuff is out there for the rancher."

Hank laid down for a nap and Dana crawled back in bed. She felt drained. When she woke up at noon, Buck came in and sat on the bed he said, "Do you believe Billie tried to do something to me?" Dana, "Ah—what can I say—yes—I think she slipped you something called a roofie or maybe I should say a date rape drug." Buck shocked, "Why and how do you know about this drug." Dana hesitant, "Well because someone did it to me once, but I still managed to walk out of a bar and get in my car driving ten miles home. I looked and acted just like you did last night. That's why I didn't take you to the hospital.

I thank God everyday that I drove my own car that night." Buck kept shaking his head, "I can't get my mind around this." "Well, Dana said, "I actually think she was going to try something with me, but I held onto my drink and we don't know this for sure. You might just have a bad case of flu."

CHAPTER 34

THAT NIGHT IT WAS just Hank and Dana home they talked about the convention, Hank wanted to know everything that went on and how people looked and what did they have to say about him?" Dana told him, "Everything she could think of and that everyone asked about him. She tried to convey to Hank the respect for him the other ranchers had shown." Hank said, "I'm ready for bed, it's been a long week." Dana, "Me too, I'll help you let's get your wheelchair. You have walked enough today." Dana was getting ready to help Hank when she heard her patio door open; she knew the back door was locked, in rushed Rosa with her children and two young Mexican girls. They all were crying so hard, trying to talk. Dana confused, "Rosa I can't understand. She was talking in both Spanish and English, slow down." Rosa took a breath and said, "The girls were being held in a house up the road. They are illegal aliens. A man named Damon Hutt had brought them here so the lady at the house could teach them English and how to do jobs in America. He told them he would get them green cards, but until they got the cards if the police caught them they would be locked in jail for months until they got deported. Dahlia has a cell phone she kept hidden so every Saturday night she called her mother. Only tonight her mother told her they had to get away because this Damon Hutt shot and killed Dahlia's cousin and threw her in a well. He tried to shoot another girl, Senna Lopez, but she got away and stole stuff to get home to Mexico. Then she told the Mexican police all about him and the people helping him. He took their cousin and this Senna to a fancy house and tried to force them to have sex with men that came to this house. When they fought with him he shot the ones that wouldn't obey. These two girls are Dahlia and Rae. I know Dahlia's father is some relation of Manuel's." Dana stood shocked and looked to Rosa, "How in the world did they get here?" Rosa shaking, "They went to the housekeeper, she's my cousin. She brought them to my house, but she ran away she needs her job. She thought a white woman like you could help because people don't believe us Mexican women." The girls both started sobbing, "They will come for us. They watch all the time. My mother said she could get to the border. If you could please get us there to meet her, she would pay you. You see, we don't know where we are." Dana trying to take all this in said, "Mikala, lock all the doors—okay—Rosa ask the girls if they are taking drugs, pills or whatever?" Rosa whirled on Dana, "You did know—you did—I knew you saw something, why did you lie?" Dana yelled back, "I knew Rosa what could I do I'm the new guy here. Did you call Manuel and are the men coming home and did you call 911?" Rosa furious, "I called the men, but Sheriff Bob he's no good I told him before about drugs—nothing—he will do nothing." Dana pulling her hair, "Rosa, this is a new ballgame we're talking murder here, I'm calling." Dana told the 911 operator the whole story as fast as she could. She told 911 that she was leaving her cell phone on so they could hear, but she asked if they heard her being threatened to just listen." Rosa was running from window to window screaming she said, "I see them coming, there's those four wheelers and a car with a spot light and people running here." Hank said," Dana get my pistol from the closet and the shells. You kids stay in my room, shut the door." After grabbing Hank's pistol Dana went and got the shotgun. She put the cell phone under the kitchen counter. Someone started knocking on the front door. By now, Dana was standing with her back against the refrigerator, facing the front door. Someone kept kicking the door until it crashed open. Dana looked at the man holding a gun, she thought—MY God—Billie's pilot is Damon Hutt. Oh my God. She said, What the Hell do you think you're doing?" He said, I'm sorry to bother you, but I have a little problem. I was trying to help our housekeeper get her children to America, their illegal and I shouldn't have tried, but she was so lonely. Anyway, the damn kids ran off. I don't know what scared them. God, I was just trying to help." He sounded so convincing, "I thought of Rosa, maybe they went to visit her, but her house was empty. The lights were on, but nobody was home there." Rosa spit at him, "In my house, you devil, you monster."

Dana said, "It's alright Rosa. We'll get this straightened out.' Damon looked at Rosa with his cold blue eyes laughing "So I'm a devil now, what's that about?" Dana's instinct told her he must not find out he was being accused of murder. He wouldn't be so cocky, if he knew what the young girls had told about him. The back door was kicked in as they all stood looking at each other like the O.K. corral. Dana with her shotgun pointed at Damon. Someone was going through the rooms. A man hollered, "I can't find them Damon, but I know they're here. I seen a slipper by the back door. He opened the door to Hank's room. Hank held the gun up, the man put his hands in the air—Hank stayed right behind him. All of a sudden Billie and Connie West came huffing and puffing in then came to a skidding halt, when they saw Dana with the gun. For a minute it threw Dana off, she suspected them doing drugs, but murder. She thought I have to keep this gun steady and I have to make them believe I will shoot. Billie said, "Nursey, you just can't seem to stay out of trouble, do you have my girls here? What the f—are you trying to pull? This is none of your business." Damon keeping his eye on Dana, "She has the girls. For some reason she thinks she is protecting them." Billie scorn in her voice, "You're going to shoot all of us—ha—I doubt it. Get out of the way while we handle this." She stopped walking when she seen Hank with a gun too. Buck, Sid, and Manuel came through the garage door—Rosa ran to Manuel, than the kids ran, flying out of the bedroom to their Dad. Rosa was already explaining in fast Spanish to Manuel, crying she kept pointing at Damon. Manuel looked at Damon, "Is this true?" Damon looking at Manuel, "What's true, I'll put my gun down, I kind of forgot I had it with me, never know there are snakes everywhere." Dana shook her head at Manuel, he caught on not to say any more. Buck horrified, "Dana, put the gun down these folks are our neighbors. What the hell is the matter with you?" Dana didn't take her eyes off Damon. She said to Buck, "NO." Finally Buck noticed the door had been kicked in. He looked totally confused by now. Dana could see behind Damon a typical Sheriff type, neat uniform, star on the front of his shirt and what looked like a deputy behind him, same uniform only no star. The sheriff said to Dana, "You can put the gun down now." Dana eyes still on Damon, "NO." Buck yelled at Dana, "Dana, this is Sheriff Bob and his deputy from Sunbird—good God put the gun down." Dana once again said, "NO."

Then Hank rolled out with his pistol on the other man, the two young girls clinging to Hank's chair. They rushed to Dana trying to get behind her. Hank, gun in hand said to Buck, "Leave her be." Buck and Sid looked from Dana to Hank shock on their faces. Another polic. man came striding in behind Damon, he had on a different uniform, but it was obvious he was police. He had a gun in a holster off his shoulder, tall, quiet, calm, chewing gum. Damon looked at the new guy and told his story again about how lonely his housekeeper was and he brought her two girls in illegally. He just wanted to help. Rosa and the two girls screamed, "Liar." The new gum chewing cop said to the Sheriff, "Bob, can we use your office and have everyone tell their side of this story." Damon swore, "oh F—what a damn mess over nothing." Sheriff Bob looking at Dana, "Okay girl, put down the gun and everyone follow me to town—Damon, Connie and Billie ride with me and we can get this straightened out. Girls you ride with my deputy." Dana yelled, "No, these two girls only go with Rosa and me—Manuel—Hank says take his car. I'm not letting these girls out of my sight. I have promised their mother that they—WILL BE HOME TONIGHT. If any of you want to mess with me and try to lock the girls up for being illegal's, you will hear from my attorney. I doubt you will play games with him." The new gum chewing, Clint Eastwood, type cop, asked Dana to look at something. He walked past her gun and with what looked like an I-Pad or big phone he typed the word Senna. Then he typed in we know and showed another picture of a girl obviously dead. The two young girls standing on either side of Dana started screaming and ran to Manuel nearly climbing up his body. Gum chewing Clint Eastwood said, "I'd like to drive you, the girls and Rosa with me so Rosa can interpret. Will you do that?" Dana put down the gun and took out the shells, looking good old Clint in the eye she said, "I'm going to grab some clean clothes and my purse. I will ride with you, but Manuel will follow and he knows to call Don Santiago if you don't do what you say." The gum chewer saluted Dana, "Yes ma'am, I agree, but leave the shotgun here—okay?"

Billie was starting to follow the Sheriff out the door when she turned and said to the tall Clint Eastwood, "I don't know who you are." He smiled at her. "My name's Patrick Dodd." She said, "Whatever, I want everyone in this room to know we have done nothing wrong—pointing at Dana—she will try anything to make me look bad so she can get her hooks into Hank Boldt Jr. She is crazy I'm surprised, pointing to Buck and Hank that she didn't shoot you in your bed some night." Rosa started to cross the room with her hands in fists. Dana eyes were like flashes of lightening, her eyes bored right into Billie's eyes and for a minute Billie looked scared then she grabbed the deputies' arm, and she turned to look one more time at Dana surprise on her face. Rosa looked at Dana, "So you can get mad after all, well, well." Buck and Sid looked embarrassed.

The Sheriff escorted Damon, Connie, Billie and the breakin man to his car. He acted all friendly to them, like this is a joke.

Buck held his hand out to Dana, "What are you doing, this is crazy?" Dana shrugged off his hand still mad, her clothes in her hand she went out to the waiting car. On the porch stood two other men—FBI written on their jackets, she stopped in her tracks turning back she said, "Hank Boldt and his son do not know what's going on. Believe me they don't have anything to do with this."

Patrick Dodd opened the car door in front for the terrified girls. Then he opened the back door and waited for Dana and Rosa. Dana looked back to make sure Manuel was behind them. Rosa had told him to take their children to her mother's house. Mr. Dodd asked the girls to start telling their story. He explained he was going to tape their story from the car to the Sunbird office and someone there would have it typed up so they could sign it. I'm kind of in a hurry because you see I will be escorting Damon Hutt by airplane to Las Vegas where I guarantee you he will be locked up. A sigh of relief came from all the occupants of the car.

Dana changed clothes by now. She didn't give a damn about anything, she felt sick at the disappointed look on Buck and Sid's faces. After Rosa and the girls told Dodd what they knew, he said, "And Rosa you need to forgive Sheriff Bob. It has taken two months to get a search warrant for Billie and Connie's house. He did believe you about the drugs and I suspect your nurse can tell us more." Dana was starting to calm down she said, "I went to a party at West's just a few days ago, the hired helps eyes were dilated, everybody was sniffing and they were happy, happy riding high. Oh, God Rosa, Eva, oh God, sir are they searching their place right now?" "Yes, I'm sorry; who is Eva? Is that the old lady that lives there?" Dana, "Can we call Mr. Boldt and have her brought to his house. Maybe her foreman could bring her?" Good old Clint picked up his phone talking to Dana, "I think we can do that. I left a couple of men at the Boldt ranch just in case some more bad apples shake loose. I'll call and have one of them go get her." He called someone and they said a man named Russ brought an elderly lady to the Boldt ranch. Was that alright?" "Affirmative." Then he said to the girl's. It is time to call your Mama's. He handed the phone to Dahlia. There were a lot of joyful happy sounds coming from the phone.

Clint cop looked over his shoulder at Dana, "You dressed yet? Okay, now I will tell you and Rosa some things, but I'm warning you. No, I think ordering you not to talk to reporters about this until after a Grand Jury meets. Will you follow my orders?" All four women in the car shook their heads—yes. Now we think we have managed to catch all the people involved in this human trafficking mess. The prettiest girls and boys were doped and sent to be prostitutes in Hutt's gentlemen clubs in Las Vegas. The not so attractive kids were eventually given jobs in his legitimate hotels, however, they had to give over thirty three percent of their wages which technically kept them slaves and of course you seen how well the bosses lived, luxury. Everything had to be the best for them." Tears were running down Rosa and Dana's faces, when they got to the Sunbird office.

Dodd brought them through the back door of the police station to what looked like an employee lunch room. Manuel must have hurried because he came right in behind them and behind him Buck walked in. Buck came right over to Dana and put his hands on her shoulder as she sat down. Dodd was showing the girls where to sign after Rosa read the report to them. Dana looked up at Buck and took his hand, "Mr. Dodd, I keep wanting to call you Clint Eastwood—ah—I know this will make Buck mad, but I have to tell you something else. The Halls who live East of Bolt's—well—I think they might be mixed up in this too. You see Dee Hall's mother's name is Stella Hutt." He leaned back and laughed, "Maybe you should be working for us. Yes, you're right. They were picked up just before we got your call." Dana worried, "What happened to the children?" He said, "Their Grandma was still there and she hopped on the first plane out with the kids. She was devastated and yet I thought she seemed relieved it was over, She must have known they were up to no good." Buck pacing back and forth, "You're telling me all my neighbors were doing this. Dad said they were killing girls, too. I can't believe Connie and Billie and Hall's—my God." Dana looked at him disgusted. You must have wondered where all their money came from. You know, no ranch paid for all that." Buck confused said, they told me their husbands died and left them lots of money." Dana went, "Really Buck, really they were stoned every time I seen them. Well, maybe you didn't know. After last night I guess you maybe didn't catch on. At least I know you can't handle drugs", then she laughed. Dodd laughed, "Ah, so you were jealous." Dana pointed her finger at him started to say something, stopped looked at Buck, "You might be right, yeah that's possible. She hugged Buck, and he's just as pretty inside as he is outside, arms crossed pointing once again at Dodd and just what are you anyway, who do you work for? You still remind me of good old Clint." He said, "Go ahead make my day! Oh, that's funny. I mean considering it was you holding a shotgun." Dana laughed then serious she asked, "Where did they take Billie and Connie?" He said, "I had better explain to you and Rosa why Sheriff Bob was being so friendly. We didn't want a fuss arresting them. By the time they got to El Paso, they were convinced Bob was pretending to talk to them. That's when my men handcuffed them and got them ready for a plane ride to Las Vegas. This Senna Lopez is the only survivor who can really tell us what each person in their sex rings job was, because she is one brave little girl, she got away. And to answer your question I am a federal investigator who handles cases like this that cross state lines and country boundaries. I am with the immigration department most of the time. Now get your little chicks home mama hen."

Manuel drove Dahlia and Rae, sat in front between Rosa and Manuel. Dana and Buck sat in back. Rosa interpreted the girl's story to Buck. Manuel found a drive through fast food place; they were all starved by now.

At the border there were police cars and a white news van. Dana warned Rosa and the girls again they were not to talk. The girls ran to their mothers. It looked to Dana, from all the cars and people there, that their whole town came to meet them. Manuel and Rosa hugged everyone. Dana laid low in the back seat; Buck looked at her like, what now? She said, "Once before I was involved in a court case I was threatened, harassed. It made my life miserable, I'm not going through that again." When Manuel got back in the car Dana offered to drive,

"I'm used to staying up all night with patients." Manuel said, "I am so happy I don't feel tired at all."

Home finally, there were still lights on in the ranch house. Sid was sitting at the table with a young FBI agent talking. They both wanted to know how the trip to the border went. Rosa and Manuel went home. The FBI agent said, "He felt they would be safe now. He thought he would go back to town and catch up on some sleep. Russ was asleep on the couch; Martha was sleeping in the recliner chair by Hanks bed and Eva was in Dana's bed. Sid trying to talk quiet said, "What a damn mess, I called Don Santiago when I found out the federal government would sell everything the West's owned even if it was Eva's place. Connie and Billie's names was on all of it, the land, cows, well everything so he's up there now trying to protect some of Eva's rights." Buck and Dana were in shock again, "WE never thought of that, thank God you did Sid." Dana didn't say another word. She went upstairs and climbed in bed in the pink room, too exhausted to even think about this terrible night.

CHAPTER 35

Mr. Argo, Maria, Senna, Gary and all kinds of other people sat around Saturday night, in Artie's house waiting for the call about Dahlia's rescue. When Anna finally called with the news Damon Hutt was in jail, they all clapped and cheered. It was late when Anna called and she quickly explained that some American white woman had held a gun on Damon until the police got there and they would be talking to her again and then Anna would have more information.

The next morning Maria and Senna arrived at work to find the parking lot full. They couldn't believe their eyes. A young woman hurried up to Senna, "I am a reporter for a reputable magazine, we want to interview you, and we will pay you lots of money for an exclusive interview." Senna told her, "I can't talk about it, there's a court order sealing my lips." The girl said, "I know that, but when it's lifted would you call me first? I will give you my card." Maria and Senna still talking to the girl did not realize they were being surrounded by people with cameras. They both put their hands over their eyes from all the flash's going off. A woman and man came and threw their arms around Maria and Senna they said, "We are FBI agents here to protect you. We wish you had stayed at home, but your boss says he desperately needs you because of all the news people staying in the hotel." Mr. and Mrs. Tate said, "We can't keep up, thank God you're here. Maria can you help in the kitchen and Senna please can you help I know those police guys don't want you here." Senna calmly put on her apron walked into the dining room stood on a chair and yelled for attention, "You can ask all the questions you want, but no one is going to tell you anything. There is a court order that I am not allowed to talk to anyone except a federal agent. Now we have food and I will get orders from you as soon as I can." The two FBI agents asked for aprons and they worked right alongside of Senna. Actually at the end of the busy day they told Senna they enjoyed it.

The next three days were like a blur to Senna. Carlotta's funeral was a circus of news people—bewildered towns people were surprised to find themselves on T.V. that night. It was a sad funeral.

At the lunch after the funeral Gary with his arm around Senna said, "Senna, you need to get out of here. I'll get plane tickets, come stay with me. You will be safe there." Senna looked at him, "Of course, I'm going home with you, but we are taking the little car. It has to go where ever I go and I do not want to spend one day away from you ever again." Gary thought this has to be the happiest day of my life. Senna packed the little car full that night and hugged her mother goodbye and drove off in a cloud of dust with Gary at her side.

CHAPTER 36

SUNDAY MORNING DANA WOKE up to the smell of bacon and eggs, she stumbled out of bed to find Eva, Hank and Buck up sitting at the kitchen table while Russ cooked a cowboy breakfast. Buck said, "The road up to Eva's is like a freeway. My God, the news vans and police cars and then there's the lookie—lou's. I ran one news guy with a camera out of here this morning. I told him this was the wrong ranch and thank God for once Bo finally decided to act like a real watch dog and ran another guy off."

Don Santiago came in for breakfast and to talk to Eva and Russ, he told them, "He could protect a lot of her assets, but maybe not the house. Russ, could she live at the bunk house with you for a while until I get this straightened out? Also Russ I think I laid the ground work for you to buy what part of the ranch you can afford maybe the south half. I'm going to talk to Sid and Buck today and see if you two would want the north half that borders your ranch." Buck told him they would talk about it and he told Russ maybe they could work out a deal on the cattle.

Days later after everything was kind of back to normal, Dana and Buck were sitting on the porch talking over all the things that had happened. Dana was worried about flying to Las Vegas to testify to a Grand Jury. Rosa couldn't wait to go, but Dana was dragging her feet. Senna Lopez had called Dana and they talked an hour. Dana trying to understand Senna's broken English, still enjoyed visiting with Senna. Senna had invited Dana to stay at Gary's house or one of his relatives. Dana said, "Buck is coming with me, Rosa and Manuel are staying with some of you, I think. I think we will get a hotel room close to the courthouse." Senna said, "I do want all of us to get together at

Gary's house. My mother is coming and Gary's mother are planning on a big meal for everyone." Dana happy to hear they would all meet said, "Oh, that sounds wonderful." Dana and Buck were both thinking back to that wild night. Then Buck laughed, "Did I tell you after Don Santiago fell in love with Eva's house, he decided to buy; furniture and all. Then he asked Sid if he could afford the half that borders our land. Sid told him I guess I have that pretty well worked out. I have good credit. Don said, "Do you need help with money?" Sid said" No, but I was kind of hoping you would throw your daughter in the deal". I guess Sid realized how awful that sounded and embarrassed he apologized. Don slapped his leg and roared," I like you and I plan on you and Lucia living in that huge house and caring for Eva until the day she dies." Sid about fainted, but he headed right up to the house and asked Lucia what she thought about all this. She looked at him like he was nuts. She said, "I already brought a lot of your clothes here I never planned on living here without you." In the quiet of the night Dana and Buck laughed. Then Buck serious took Dana's hand, "Dana should we get married? I could buy the Halls place." Dana shuddered, "Married you bet, but not the Hall place. What's wrong with living right here?" Buck chuckled in the dark, what Dana didn't know was he was flying all of her family to Texas for the weekend. He had bought a ring and wanted her girls here when he gave it to her.

CHAPTER 37

DANA WAS SHOCKED WHEN her family drove up with Sid and Manuel. She kept laughing and crying, hugging her girls and her beloved grandchildren. Buck grilled steaks and hot dogs that night and the next morning Lucia, Rosa and Martha had a breakfast brunch ready, at Lucia's beautiful home. Sid took everyone horseback riding in the morning, the afternoon they all enjoyed Lucia's heated pool. That night Buck had rented the backroom of the lounge in town. Rosa and Lucia had fixed it all up and everyone was told it was going to be a dressed up party. Dana did finally put on her long red dress and jewelry. After they ate Buck said he had an announcement to make; he pulled the ring out of his pocket and held Dana's hand while he put it on her finger, she sat stunned for one minute than crying she grabbed Buck and kissed him then ran around the room showing everybody her ring. The next day they toured the ranch and then it was time for Dana's family to go home. She did cry when they were getting on the plane, but knew she was right where she wanted to be forever.

CHAPTER 38

THE GRAND JURY WAS still ahead making Dana nervous. Senna had Gary's children teaching her English so she could pass the test to become an American citizen, the kids loved her it made them feel so important to be teaching an adult. Buck, Dana, Manuel and Rosa flew to Las Vegas for the Grand Jury the next day. Gary, Senna, Dahlia and Rae met them at the airport, Dahlia and Rae jumped up and down with excitement first they ran to Rosa and then to Dana showering her with hugs. Maria, Mary and Anna Gonzales had prepared a huge meal. Senna introduced her mother and Mr. Argo. Clara Ring and her husband came to supper along with Barry and Nina. It was quite a crowd everyone with a story to tell—it was like a jig saw puzzle each of them carried a piece to bring down a Human Trafficking Ring. The next morning Patrick Dodd and the prosecuting attorney met with all of them at a breakfast buffet place. He explained, what would happen today, that only one at a time would go in the court room to give their testimony. They was driven to the courthouse in police vans for their own safety. Dana and Senna were both nervous about seeing Damon Hutt and Patrick seemed to know that. He told the two of them they were too tender-hearted and then told them all the other murders Damon was involved in. It took all day for all the witnesses to go in. Senna was first, and then the other girls. When it came time for Rosa, she couldn't wait, the anger in her eyes to finally see Connie and Billie get what's coming to them she said. Dana on the stand did manage to get in that she did not believe Dee and Ned Hall or Connie and Billie West knew about the murders.

That night Patrick Dodd took them all out to eat and then on to his own house for drinks and dessert. He lived in a gorgeous house, on a hill overlooking the bright lights of Las Vegas.

They were all so relieved to have the Grand Jury over with; they were like one big happy family all of them decided to stay longer and take in all the Las Vegas sights.

Dana invited all of them to visit the ranch sometime and she told them that she knew Lucia would love to have them, too.

CHAPTER 39

SENNA HAD NO IDEA that in a few months she would be a wealthy woman with news interviews and invitations to talk shows. She would become a household name throughout the whole world. Gary would handle her money; they had decided to build a new house at the lake. Senna wanted to be close to Clara Ring, who became her second mother; she did study hard and became an American citizen. She moved her mother and Mr. Argo, who had married, to a new house in Las Vegas. Lupe and Nika moved to Mr. Argo's farm and became quite prosperous.

Hank Boldt moved to Martha's ranch where he spent his days fixing things around the house and gardening. They bought a new motorhome and traveled whenever they felt like it.

Rosa had her baby. Pete vanished never to be seen again.

Damon Hutt, Mary Belle and George were sentenced to life in prison for murder.

Connie, Billie and the Halls were doing long sentences for fraud, promoting prostitution, and money laundering.

The people involved in helping to solve the ring of Human Trafficking become best friends through phone calls, e-mails and visits to the ranch. Senna and Gary came when ever Senna was giving a talk in Texas on the sex trade, to stay with either Dana or Lucia. Dana often thought that it took a violent act of murder to bring all of them together, she cherished the times they spent together.

Dana and Buck stayed on the ranch; they did everything together, Dana took over a lot of Pete's work she became an expert horse woman. Dana and Lucia put together a three day gala event for their cattle customers; it was a very profitable success. Dana thanked God everyday for her wonderful life and that God brought so much good from such terrible evil.